I0521424

Storylandia

The Wapshott Journal of Fiction

Issue 27

The Wapshott Press

Storylandia, Issue 26, The Wapshott Journal of Fiction, ISSN 1947-5349, ISBN 978-1-942007-21-0 is published at intervals by the Wapshott Press, now a 501(c)(3) nonprofit, PO Box 31513, Los Angeles, California, 90031-0513, telephone 323-201-7147. All correspondence can be sent to The Wapshott Press, PO Box 31513, LA CA 90031-0513. Visit our website at www.WapshottPress.org to learn more.
This work is copyright © 2018 by Storylandia. The Wapshott Journal of Fiction, Los Angeles, California. Copyright © 2017 James White and is reprinted here with the copyright owner's permission.

Storylandia is always seeking quality original short stories, novelettes, and novellas. Please have a look at our submission guidelines at www.Storylandia.WapshottPress.org or email the editor at editor@wapshottpress.org

Cover: Warsaw, Poland post-WWII

Storylandia

The Wapshott Journal of Fiction

Founded in 2009

Issue 27, Autumn 2018

Edited by Ginger Mayerson

Vistula

By James White

Copyright © 2017 By James W. White

Vistula is a work of fiction. Names, characters, businesses, places, events and locales are either the products of the author's imagination or used in a fictitious manner. Any resemblance to actual persons, living or dead, or to actual events is purely coincidental. The training incident described as taking place at Slapton Sands, England, was a factual event, officially called Exercise Tiger. Communication problems and a German attack during the exercise resulted in the deaths of at least 749 American servicemen.

Acknowledgment

Thanks to Michael James Fitzpatrick and his pop rock concept album, Love And Hate, about three brothers who fought for the American armed forces during World War II. My collaboration with Michael, writing the story for Love And Hate, became the inspiration for Vistula.

Vistula

by
James White

VISTULA

On a river bank near Warsaw

THEY LINED US ALONG THE TOP OF A STEEP RIVER BANK, a long drop above the river. Thirty of us faced the water, hands tied behind our backs with wire. The men around me coughed, cried and prayed, making low murmuring noises, barely audible. It was cold, of course. It's always cold in Poland. Even their pathetic summers are a joke compared to Pennsylvania's hot sultry days.

Across the river, lights from the few buildings still standing in the Zoliborz district twinkled in the weak winter twilight. Shadows hid the bombed-out neighborhoods, the smoke, the smoldering ruins. The pop, pop, pop of small arms fire broke the stillness. I instinctively identified the weapon, a Strumgewehr 44. The sound was strangely comforting, knowing I wasn't the target.

Blue chunks of ice bumped and grated against each other in the swift current below me. The river would be frozen solid by now if it weren't for the tons of war waste and chemicals. When the sun reflected off the river just right, the water took on the green tint of anti-freeze.

Listening to the ice, I shut my eyes and composed myself, thinking about my last day at home.

My two brothers and I were skylarking and fooling around downtown Allentown. It was early December, Sunday, the seventh, 1941, and it was beginning to snow.

We'd said we were going Christmas shopping. Papa told us to watch out for pickpockets while mama cautioned us to behave. When we got off the trolley, we saw an Army recruiting office.

While we sat on benches outside Leopold's Deli with greasy Polish dogs in our hands, everything changed. News about Pearl Harbor came from the deli's radio. While my brothers argued about what to do next, I ran to that recruiting office and never looked back.

Allentown

"WHERE'D THAT COME FROM?" Me and my brothers were on our way to town and I'd gone ahead, mingling with a crowd of families on their way to church. I stopped to stare– a little kid bumped into me. Her mom apologized and gave the kid's arm a jerk. I paid no attention, because my eyes were riveted on the Army recruiting office across the street from the courthouse on Hamilton Street.

It used to be Dominico's Five and Dime. Now it was all lit up with soldiers inside and people milling around the door. A poster in the front window claimed, 'Uncle Sam Wants YOU.' Considering the season, Uncle Sam kinda looked like Santa Claus, but without the cheery smile.

Most of the shops in downtown Allentown were closed, on account of it being Sunday, but the main streets were all lit up and there was enough going on to keep us occupied.

It started to snow. I pulled down the brim of my cap and buttoned my argyle sweater. My girlfriend, Rosie, had given me the matching sweater and cap for my seventeenth birthday. They weren't especially warm, but they meant a lot to me. Rosie kissed me when she gave me the package. Right in front of my parents and brothers. I got a lot of ribbing about that later, but I could tell both brothers were impressed. Impressed and jealous.

The aroma of grilled onions coming from down the street made my mouth water, even though it was still officially morning.

"Peanut! Where are you?" My brothers shouted from a block away. Albert and Theo Zewiski were both older and stronger than me. Al, the eldest, was nineteen. Six feet tall, he was the pride of the family. Theo, eighteen, was shorter, but he made up for his shrimpy, skinny frame with a mischievous mind and a flair for sadism.

We had planned to leave right after the eight a.m. Sunday Mass, but Mama made us come home first and have some breakfast. "Save you some money," she said over a skillet popping with fried eggs and bacon. "Otherwise, you'll be hungry as soon as you get there and waste your money on food instead of Christmas presents."

I had to chuckle. That was the story all of us agreed on to keep the peace. Otherwise, our parents would never approve of us wasting our time and money on foolishness like arcade games and Polish sausages from Leopold's, especially Papa.

The old man rocked in his chair, a cup of coffee in one hand, his pipe in the other, while we gobbled up our food. "Back in the old country, we didn't have a town to go to, much less any money to waste," he said, pointing his pipe at us.

'Back in the old country' was Papa's favorite thing to say about anything we did that he disapproved of.

Theo never missed an opportunity to rebel. "Back in the blah, blah, blah," he mumbled, crouched over his plate so Papa couldn't hear.

Mama did, but she rolled her eyes and pretended not to notice.

The old country was a mysterious place to me. My brothers too, or so they said. We knew the name of the town where Mama and Papa grew up, we celebrated the big Catholic holidays with Polish embellishments and we'd learned a few Polish words, but that was it. Mama insisted we speak English in the house and 'be American.'

We'd been talking more about Poland since the German invasion. Mama cried sometimes when she read letters from her sister in Warsaw. We knew Papa's uncle had died while fighting the German army, but Mama said we should never to bring it up.

After breakfast, Albert and Theo had to promise they'd keep an eye on me.

"Keep little Johnny safe and don't let him out of your sight," Mama had shouted from the kitchen.

I cringed and avoided eye-contact with my brothers. We stood in the doorway, itching to take off. Theo jabbed me in the back and made a smirking noise.

"Yes, Mama," Al said. "All we're going to do is some Christmas shopping."

Papa sucked on his pipe and scowled. He knew Christmas shopping was the last thing on our minds. "Stay out of the way of those cops," he'd said. He cast a firm stare at Theo. "And you stay out of trouble."

We promised to be home before dinner.

"Look out for pick-pockets!" was the last thing I heard Papa say as we raced around the corner toward the trolley stop.

"HEY PIPSQUEAK," Al shouted a second time. "We can't see you!"

I kept quiet and concentrated on the recruiting office. You gotta be eighteen. They'll kick me out on my butt the minute I walk in the door. I sighed, then caught sight of Theo.

"There you are." Theo dashed around a line of children holding hands, all dressed in their Sunday best, and grabbed my shoulder. He followed my stare and regarded the recruiting poster. "You gotta be kidding..."

Al grabbed my other shoulder. His grip tighter than Theo's. "Whaddya think you're doin'?" Al was breathing hard. I knew he was anxious. "You get yourself lost the moment we're off the trolley?"

"I ain't lost." I shrugged the two hands off me.

Theo motioned toward the recruiting office. "He was lookin' over there."

Al studied the brightly lit storefront. "Where'd that come from?" he murmured.

"I know, right?" I said. "Just last week it was an abandoned shell. Those guys move fast."

Theo laughed. "And it'll probably be gone tomorrow."

"I wouldn't be so sure," Al replied and shook his head. He looked at me. "What are you doin' lookin' over there anyways? We're supposed to be Christmas shopping."

Theo let out with another of his heartless, mocking chuckles. He pulled my cap over my eyes. "I bet he wants to enlist. Be the hero of the family."

Al's eyes got big. "Are you crazy? You're barely seventeen, in case you've forgotten. They'd kick you out on your butt before you got through the front door."

I straightened my cap. "I look like I'm eighteen and I can lie as good as either of you."

"Like hell," Theo said. "With that stupid sweater? You look more like eight than eighteen."

"Number Two." I snarled back and punched Theo, but before I could break away, Al grabbed me around the waist and lifted me off my feet.

"Steady, little brother. You're not getting out of my sight again. What are you so hot under the collar about anyways? The Army's no place for shrimps."

"I have my reasons, and I ain't no shrimp."

The bells at Saint Stephen's Episcopal Church tolled through downtown. The jostling crowd began to hurry.

Al brushed snow off his trousers.

I glared at him and took out my handkerchief to wipe my face. I was perspiring in spite of the cold.

"It's been two years now and I've been listening to Papa talk about nothin' else besides Hitler ever since Poland was invaded. And I think it's terrible what Hitler's doing, and..."

"Wait a minute, buster." Theo tried to pull my cap over my eyes again but I dodged his hand. "Don't start dreaming about bein' the family hero. If Papa wants you to save the world, he'll tell you."

We all shut up when a girl we knew passed us on the crowded sidewalk. She was wrapped in a warm winter coat with a fur collar.

"Why, if it isn't the Zewiski brothers," she said. Her eyes lingered on Al, ignoring Theo and me.

Al nodded and flashed his disarming smile.

"What's it to ya?" Theo, growled. Eyes downcast, he turned his back on Al and the girl. "I'm hungry," he said and walked away.

I stammered a lame holiday hello and hoped the snow hid my blushing face. Standing as tall and straight as I could, I wished I brought my winter coat to make me look bigger than I was.

After the girl left, Al gestured for me to follow. "We're not having much fun standing around here."

"Hold up," I said. "I was talkin' about Mama..."

Albert stopped and gave me an impatient look over his shoulder. "What?"

"Mama cries every night when they go to bed. I hear her through the wall." I took a step back. "She told me some of her cousins were killed in the blitzkrieg. I don't care about you, but I'm tired of doin' nothing about it."

Al stood silent. The snowfall was getting heavier. He rolled his eyes and smiled.

"Okay, Peanut, you win. We'll talk it over with Mama and Papa tonight after dinner. Maybe it's time we did something."

"They'll just say no." I looked back at the recruiting office almost hidden behind falling snow and mist. "Let me just go in and ask what the deal is. I won't take a second."

"What's the big hurry? I tell ya, those guys ain't goin' anywhere." Al started walking again. "Like I said already, we'll talk to Papa first. All right?"

He gave me one of his 'end of discussion' looks. I meekly nodded.

We caught up with Theo at Wanamaker's. The shop windows were decked out with Christmas scenes and the sidewalk was crowded with gawkers.

We jostled our way through the throng, glancing at a big display of tricycles, phonograph players, dolls, model trains and mannequins dressed in grown-up men's and lady's clothes. While Al and Theo argued about which electric train set was the best, I looked back down the street, but the recruiting office was out of sight.

Al shifted his attention toward the gray, snowy sky when an airplane passed overhead, blotting out the sounds of Christmas carols and tinkling bells. Hidden in the clouds, its engines made a powerful full-throated rumble. The vague outline of a multi-engine aircraft appeared briefly, illuminated by the street lights, heading southeast.

"I bet it's one of those Boeing B-17s I been reading about. It's probably headed for the airfield in Philly." After it disappeared, Al took a deep breath and brushed snow off his face. "It has lots of guns and can carry tons of bombs and can fly in all kinds of weather—"

"So what?" Theo retorted.

"So, I've been thinking about maybe joining the Army Air Corps. I heard lots of guys are joining up to help the British. They need pilots."

"Fly airplanes?" Theo looked at his brother, put his hand to his mouth and gave him a mock expression of surprise. "You never said anything."

"Always wanted to," Albert said. He turned away and continued looking in the window. I could tell he was a little embarrassed. Theo could embarrass anybody.

"You won't find me in one of those death traps," Theo shook his head. "No room for error, people shootin' at 'ya and the consequences of a mistake are fatal every time. No siree, not for me."

"Can it," Al said without looking at his brother. "They got parachutes. Lots of guys bail out of disabled planes. Happens all the time."

Theo grunted. "Out of the frying pan into the fire, if you ask me. I bet a lot of those parachute guys wind up impaled on the end of a telephone pole."

Al withdrew into a menacing silence.

I sensed trouble brewing, so I piped up. "I'm joining the Army. Stayin' on good ol' terra-firma. Maybe in a fox hole one night and in a captured chateau the next. I'm gonna help liberate Poland from the Nazis, just like Mama wants–"

"Will you shut up about the Army?" Theo cut me off. "Enough war stories. I'm hungry."

I punched him. "Just 'cause you don't have any plans, Number Two."

Theo shoved a handful of snow down the back of my neck. I turned and kicked him.

"I do so have plans," he answered. "They're just not all about armies and bombardiers and war." He pointed up the street at a grill set up on the sidewalk outside our favorite deli. Sausages popped and spit over red coals.

"You idiots can share your war dreams. I plan on having one of those. Maybe two."

It was our favorite deli because it had a Polish name, Leopold's, which happened to be Papa's name. I bet Leopold's food wasn't any different than all the other delis in Allentown, but we wouldn't eat anywhere else.

When we stood around the grill, we heard a radio announcer inside talking in a shrill voice about casualties and damage at an American Naval base called Pearl Harbor. The base was on an island somewhere in the Pacific Ocean. There was a lot of static and he kept talking about Japan and a sneak attack. The customers in the deli were quiet. Even the Salvation Army guy on the sidewalk stopped ringing his bell and had his head in the deli's front door.

"What's happening, Peter?" Al said to the cook as he poked at the grill, full of kielbasa, bacon and buns warming along the sides.

Peter was a big guy. He stood impassively in a grimy tee-shirt, sweating over the coals and smoking a cigarette. The falling snowflakes melted immediately as they hit him. He shrugged his shoulders and never looked up. "Who cares. Not in my neighborhood. You want sauerkraut with that?"

We all nodded and glanced at each other, worried looks on our faces. Something dreadfully wrong was happening, but we didn't know what it was all about.

We took our food to a bench in front of the hardware store, two stores down. The street sounds had changed. The Christmas atmosphere was missing. Half-way through our dogs, Al grunted and looked at Theo. "So where's Pearl Harbor, mister know-it-all."

"Hawaii," Theo said, sauerkraut juice and mustard dribbling out the corner of his mouth. "It's an island in the Pacific Ocean. They got volcanoes. I saw pictures in the National Geographic Magazine. The women do this dance called the hula-hula. They wear grass skirts with no tops." Theo looked at me like he was sharing a sinister secret. "Didn't Mister Larson teach you that in geography?"

"No tops?" Al scratched his head. "I think I'd remember that." He looked back at the deli. "I guess it's a big deal. That announcer sure is excited."

I didn't know what to think. Why were the Japanese bombing our Navy base? I thought they were fighting the Chinese. I wondered if any of the ladies in grass skirts got hurt. The thought of bombs exploding in the middle of a bunch of ladies dancing the hula-hula with no tops made me squirm.

People on the sidewalk had stopped strolling and were talking to each other in huddled clumps.

"We ought to think about going home," Al said. "Find out what Papa knows."

Theo shook his head. "Keep your shirt on. I'm still eating, damn it."

"Don't say damn it!" Al lashed back at Theo. I knew he was still smarting from Theo mocking his airplane pilot dreams.

"I'll say whatever I want to say, flyboy. You can fly all the way to grandma's house as far as I'm concerned."

The two of them stood up and glared at each other.

I'd lost my appetite. The greasy wax paper, streaked with mustard and pieces of grilled onion, looked ugly and my stomach turned at the sight.

While my brothers postured and argued, I spotted a trashcan in front of the deli.

"I'm gonna toss this and pee," I said. Not waiting for an answer, I jogged back to the deli. I didn't dare look back.

That's when I knew I had my chance. Something serious was happening, getting people all excited and doin' stuff they wouldn't ordinarily do. Time to make my move.

The deli customers were still frozen, engrossed in the announcer's screechy voice. I took one last look back when I slipped in the front door.

Theo kept his face trained on his big brother. Al glanced in my direction. I thought I saw a hint of sadness in his eyes, like he understood what I had to do, but he didn't say anything.

Quick as a cat, I ran through the deli and out the back door of the kitchen which led to the alley.

I smiled as I cut through the cars crawling along Hamilton Street in the heavy snow. *I may never get this chance again.* The feeling of freedom was intoxicating.

Safely on the other side, the memory of my brothers dissolved into ghosts like the silhouettes walking along the sidewalk, miles from me now. "Tell Mama and Papa I love them," I murmured. "I'll be right back."

Claptown

I SHOULD HAVE LISTENED TO THEO.

In three months I was transformed from a shrimp into a soldier. Basic Training and Advanced Infantry Training happened while I waited in endless lines and adjusted to a physically demanding, communal life-style where my most private affairs were the subject of endless banter. But at least I wasn't alone. My fears were shared by men, not boys, who slept and ate and laughed and cried next to me, all of them just as afraid as I was.

When our company marched across the parade grounds on graduation day, I became Private Zewiski. I was still short and skinny, my wavy blond hair was nothing more than a buzz cut and my big Polish nose was just as big, but now I was a proud member of the United States Army. I looked to my left as we passed our commander in review and smiled as he saluted us. I was part of a dedicated team, all of us trained and prepared for war.

Or so I thought.

The enlistment officer at Allentown assured me the Army was gonna liberate Poland just as soon as we landed in war-torn Europe. I listened to his serious words and nodded enthusiastically while I signed my enlistment papers. Mama would be so proud if she saw me.

Instead of being proud, Mama pleaded with me to come home. Papa never wrote anything. My brothers scorned me for getting them into trouble. Except for Rosie, I didn't waste my time writing back.

We didn't get a Christmas leave because of Pearl Harbor. All I got was a Christmas card from Mama, and Rosie sent me a picture. The excitement that got me through training had worn off while marching in the miserable piney hills of Fort Benning. Some guys who lived close to the post got overnight passes. The rest of us had to stick it out in the barracks. The cooks made us a Christmas dinner and we toasted the new year with an endless supply of 3.2 beer at the enlisted men's club, but I was still in cold, wet Georgia.

We all cheered when our orders finally came through, but when we got off the boat in Africa instead of Europe, that's when I realized Theo had been right all along. Instead of liberating towns and villages, treated like heroes, we baked in a desert sun and huddled behind sand dunes. Our generals fretted and argued while us guys on the ground got whipped by General Rommel and his elite Afrika Korps. Things weren't working out like I figured.

I wasn't a bad soldier. I stayed on with the First Infantry Division, the Big Red One we called it, all through that African shit-hole called Tunisia and on to Sicily.

But after Sicily, when the Army reneged on its

promise a second time, I deserted. That's right, the red-blooded, all-American GI who had enlisted on the day Pearl Harbor was attacked abandoned his post while on guard duty.

Desertion is a serious offense, especially in wartime, and I knew the consequences when I turned my back on my buddies and hid under a blanket in the back seat of a beat-up Vauxhall sedan. Certain death was the consequence. I saw it done one afternoon on the road to Monte Basilio.

We got a brief respite to take a dump and open a can of C-rations. While we ate and kvetched, they'd trussed the poor bastard and stood him in front of a firing squad. Six volunteers. Some non-com read the orders. No blindfold, no drum roll, no last cigarette; just Ready, Aim, End of story. In the name of efficiency, the Army had taken away all the romance from its executions.

But I had good reasons for deserting and I'm proud to say I made it to Poland on my own, which was more than the Army ever did for me. Unfortunately, my circumstances when I got there were not favorable. I was on the run, hiding in a bramble on the outskirts of Warsaw with a squad of Nazis sniffing up my rear.

That's where Jakub found me. It was springtime, April, 1944.

WORD WAS AFTER SICILY we would proceed to France, then head East and liberate the Polish people, my people, from the Nazi extermination machine before the Ruskies packed off whoever was left to Siberia.

And I was good for that. The reason I got into this rotten war was to help my Polish cousins fight the Nazis. I had promised my mother and even though she hated me for enlisting, I wasn't going to welsh on my promise. I forgave the Army for that wild goose chase through Africa and Sicily and made ready to achieve my destiny.

Patton told us we'd be in France by November, then he left the outfit, fucking weasel.

Next thing I knew we were packed on a freighter and heading for England, of all places. Why England? We weren't even at war with England.

My buddies were all smiles. "British pussy!" they all cheered while we churned our way up the Atlantic. "Fucking cow-eyed, frigid Limeys," I said back, while Nazi occupied France disappeared over the horizon, off our right side.

When we reached England, my bad attitude was reinforced by fog, rain and mushy peas. Sunny Sicily seemed like paradise in hindsight, despite the bullets.

We were bivouacked on a beach in Dover, south England, playing beach landing games with the Brits. Training they called it. The training wasn't going to happen for weeks, so in between guard duty and close-order drill on a rocky beach, I spent my furloughs gagging down warm fucking beer in a nowhere town called Slapton, half mile from our encampment. Claptown, as those of us from first Platoon, Company B called it. After a few pints, I often spent my evenings airing my grievances to an uncaring public about being cheated out of Poland.

I WAS WELL INTO MY POLAND rant one night when a guy asked if he could take the empty seat next to me.

I gave him a careless, permissive nod. I could tell he was a Polack. Big ears, fat nose, blond with a stupid, toothy grin.

"You from the old country?" he says when I took a gulp of my beer. He was wearing civvies.

"And what the fuck do you care if I am?" I replied. I was mildly insulted, somebody calls me out about my ancestry, but I decided to be cool about it.

"No offense. You're talking about Poland. Just wondered."

I looked past him, at uniforms plus a few low-slung frocks, packed shoulder to shoulder in the smoky bar. They were playing Glenn Miller. Everybody was close, but nobody looked at each other. Claptown was a nothing, pissant hole, but these days, with us Americans around, it was buzzing with spies, pimps, informants, whores, pick-pockets, you name it, all trying to figure out what we were doing there and how they could profit from it. We were warned not to fraternize with strangers.

I set my pint glass on the bar and took a long drag on my Brit cigarette. It was an adjustment, but I had switched to Players to fit in. "I'm of Polish extraction, what of it?"

"Thought so." He held out his beefy hand. "Kurkowski. Peter Kurkowski, pleased to-"

I gripped my pint and shook my head. The acrid Players smoke stung my eyes. Things were going way too fast.

"I'll have a Flowers," he said to the barkeep. He dropped his hand as if nothing had happened. "What are you having?"

Normally, pimps and queers don't matter much to me. To each his own, I say. But to tie my homeland with a homo come-on was below the belt. I gave him my slow, side-long glance coupled with a resounding sneer. "I'm not having shit, if that's what you're asking."

A little color ran up Kurkowski's neck. "You think I'm propositioning you?"

I didn't dignify his remark with an answer.

"Please, don't be offended." He kept on talking. "It was your accent. Reminded me of home. Pojąć?"

I took a long gulp and emptied my pint, Kurkowski's Polish ringing in my ears. The barkeep looked at me and I shook my head. "Nice talkin' to ya, Kurkowski," I said as I got off my stool and lay a crown on the bar.

Two grunts hustled each other to take my seat.

In the ensuing scuffle, Kurkowski reached over, lightening fast, and stuck a small piece of paper in my breast pocket. "Likewise, I'm sure," he said.

Against my better judgment, I met up with Kurkowski four days later.

He had written my name on his piece of paper and said he had news about my Mother's family, Nowicki, in Poland. In tiny, perfect hand writing, he also said he would stop by the Saint James Church every evening at seven pm. That got me curious. No homo would go to that much trouble. I decided I needed to find out how and why he knew my name and the name of my Aunt. Enough to hazard being accused of having a deviant encounter with a civilian. Such an offense was not quite as bad as desertion, but damn close.

I'd gone by the church a few times to get the layout. It was a crumbling ruin with no discernible features except a front door and a graveyard. When I rattled the door knob, a large, black rat scurried across the threshold and into the yard. I took that as an omen.

It had rained all day and the ever-present fog and smell of coal-burning blanketed Claptown. After making appearances at the bar, I made my excuses and stumbled out.

I was so paranoid somebody would recognize me, I changed clothes. On my way to the church, I ditched my uniform in a warehouse and got into some slacks and a dress shirt. I added a fedora and a pair of fake glasses to complete the disguise.

My wet civilian clothes stuck to me while I struggled to change, hopping on one foot, grabbing a hand-hold in the dark and nearly toppling over crates of empty bottles.

Cold and uncomfortable, I made my way along the town's only paved street, avoiding the few streetlights and keeping a sharp eye out for MPs. A reprimand kept running through my head, 'Halt, soldier, what the fuck you doin'?'

"Private Zewiski."

It was his voice, but it came from nowhere. I stared into the shadows that shrouded the church door when I felt a tap on my shoulder.

"It's me, Peter."

I turned around and he pulled a hood back from his face. It was him all right, with the same toothy grin.

I had a speech and a set of demands all ready, but before I could get a word out he shook his head and put his palm in front of my face. He didn't waste time with small talk.

"Your Aunt Elzbieta is alive, but barely, living in a Warsaw apartment."

I stared back at him, bewildered, my speech forgotten. "How do you know–?"

"She's ill and her two children are being taken care of by a neighbor. I regret to report your Uncle died some months ago. Heart attack."

He paused, listening. Poised, ready to fight or flee, like a cat.

I looked around and saw nothing. "Why are you telling me this?"

Kurkowski trained his eyes back on me. "I'm associated with a Polish resistance cell. We're recruiting volunteers."

I could barely hear him. "Volunteers?" I whispered. "Did you say volunteers?"

He nodded. "We have information that you, John Zewiski, have close family relations with residents in Warsaw."

"Volunteers for what?"

Kurkowski's smile evaporated. His blue eyes gleamed in the pale light. "Warsaw is being systemically destroyed, block by block, and its inhabitants massacred. The Nazis have killed all the Jews and now they plan to level the city. Those of us that can are undertaking a resistance, but we need help. Your help."

"But me myself? What can I do? I was supposed to be there with the Army."

A movement, a rustling sound came from somewhere. "Next time eight pm," Kurkowski whispered as he pulled his hood back over his head. He turned and disappeared into the shadows that covered the grave yard.

"Is there someone out there?" A voice came from the church door. "Can I be of any assistance?" The door opened and a shaft of light stretched across the grounds. A figure in a cape stopped at the threshold and shined a flashlight.

"Damn." My heart beating hard against my chest, I turned and sprinted up the gravel path back to the road. I didn't stop or turn around until I squeezed myself into the crowded bar. The fedora and glasses I tossed in a trash bin next to the bar's door. I lost track of where my uniform was.

Civvies weren't allowed off-post, but it was a minor infraction. I figured if I was collared, I could get away with it by acting like I was embarrassed about a date with a local lass that went bad.

I stood at the bar, head down, nursing my pint. My mind spun in a thousand different directions. Aunt Elzbieta and Uncle Bazyli, now deceased. Should I write to Mother? My two cousins, helpless children caught in a raging war of annihilation. How did Kurkowski know these family details? It was too weird to believe, but what if it's true? My own flesh and blood, huddled in some bombed-out building, waiting to be the next victims. I still didn't know how or why he knew my name and the name of my Aunt. Should I take the chance to meet Kurkowski again? Was I being drawn into some sinister subterfuge?

"Zewiski." A heavy hand slammed down on my shoulder. I nearly spat out my mouthful of beer. Sputtering, I turned around and stared into the boozy, beet-red face of my sergeant.

"No civvies off post. You know the rules." Sergeant Sturgis weaved, but held steady, thanks to my shoulder. He looked me up and down. "Article fifteen offense. Wartime. No exceptions."

"Sarge," I whined. My trousers and shirt were still wet, I noticed I got the buttons wrong on my shirt and it was half un-tucked. Conversations around us lowered an octave. "She wanted me to meet her folks. All nice-like, ya know? What was I supposed to do?"

"You're supposed to wear your uniform." Sturgis gave me a wicked smile. "Changed your tune about them cow-eyed Limeys huh?" He looked at his buddy, another sergeant from A Company.

"Bust 'im," the asshole said. He leered at me. "Fer wearing civvies and for not knowing how to wear 'em. You look like a slob, Zewiski."

Sturgis rolled his eyes. "I don't want to have to fuck with the paperwork, Zewiski. Training maneuvers start tomorrow, five am. All passes are canceled. I'm putting you on guard duty for the next two weeks straight. Report to the duty officer tomorrow, eighteen-hundred hours. Got that?"

I nodded. Instead of responding, questions, strategies, contingencies swirled behind my eyes.

"Say it." Sturgis stuck his big mug straight into my face, his beer breath stinging my eyes. "Say it so's I can hear it."

Like a good soldier, I got off my stool, stood up straight, shoulders back. "Yes Sergeant!" I replied.

I needed answers, but I didn't want to wind up staring down the barrels of six standard issue, thirty-caliber M-1 rifles.

Problem was, the answers lay a half-mile from my location. How do I get there without arousing suspicion? Kurkowski, said he'd show up at the church at eight o'clock every night, but for how long? Fucking with the duty officer was a dangerous gambit, but I had a few tools I could use to facilitate a brief disappearance. Bribery was always effective, so was intimidation, plus I had a few personal leverage points I could lay on certain individuals. I weighed each option carefully while I walked back to my tent.

"Psssst, Zewiski." Behind the familiar voice, an object arched over the perimeter fence and landed a few feet in front of me. When it landed with a clang, footsteps crunched across the rocky shoreline and faded into the night.

I walked over the object and looked around. I didn't see nobody so I scooped it up in one smooth motion and stuffed it inside my tunic. A metal tin. No bigger than a pack of cigarettes.

Aunt in serious danger. Volunteers departing in one week. Leave yes/no answer. Nothing more. I wait for your reply at this place.

I studied the handwriting and compared it with the paper he gave me. It was him all right. Volunteers? So I'm not the only one? Serious danger now? What does that mean?

Yes,no,yes,no,yes,no. Such a simple answer. With so much at stake either way.

I was tempted to throw the box away. It was starting to sound too cloak and dagger to be serious, yet he knew my family's names. I couldn't explain that away. One way or another, I needed to find out.

The first few days of training maneuvers had gone miserably well. We spent our time riding LSTs in and out of the waves, marching through loose gravel with a full pack and getting soaked. After that, I would take a ride back to camp, change and march guard duty for four more hours.

Then everything went to hell. We were told to be ready for a live fire exercise. Big deal, but some idiots got the disembarkation times wrong and, while we slogged through the waves, what was supposed to be a training exercise with bullets over our heads turned into a carnage. People were getting shot all around us. We spent the rest of the day pulling wounded and dead men off the beach. And, because we were short handed, I had to do double shifts of guard duty.

After my second shift, I stumbled into my rack completely worn out, physically and emotionally. All I could think about were the poor bastards I dragged off the beach and my family being slaughtered in Warsaw. How could I come home if Mother found out her sister and children were all dead?

"Where were you, Johnny?" I could hear her say it. "You left me to save them."

The next day, as if things couldn't get worse, German submarines attacked our LSTs during another exercise. They tore up and sunk a bunch of them, leaving hundreds more men screaming and dying in the flaming water. Our camp turned into a morgue.

And to top it off, the officers ordered us to keep the screw-up a secret. No apologies, no memorial services, no chaplains, no nothing. Morale in the camp sunk to an all-time low.

While on another double-shift of guard duty, I wrote 'yes' on a scrap of paper, stuffed it in Kurkowski's box and threw it over the fence where I had found it. I was too exhausted to care anymore and what did I have to lose? A 'Yes' answer kept my options open and I could refuse once the time came.

Guard duty turned into a walking nightmare filled with visions of the cold, dead faces of men I had been drinking with just a week ago. Staggering down the fence line, I struggled to keep awake when a red signal flare zoomed skyward and burst into a cone of sparkling stars. It came from the direction of the shoreline. Immediately, shouts echoed across the compound and searchlights swept the beach. A siren wailed.

Guards were supposed to keep to their posts in the event of an incident and I stood still, rifle at ready, waiting for my eyes to adjust after watching the flare and looking for movement in the pitch black void on the other side of the fence line. The hair on the back of my neck stood up and my exhaustion was temporarily replaced by adrenaline.

"Psssst, Zewiski."

The fence jerked back and forth once, twice.

"Halt!" I shouted. I took aim at the fence. "Who goes–"

"Shush!" Came the reply.

A weak beam of light illuminated a hole in the fence at ground level. A pair of hands held the cut fence open. "Through here. Quick."

With all the hubbub going on, I had forgotten about the tin and the message and Kurkowski and Warsaw. I wasn't prepared to make a decision. "I don't know, Kurkowski." I bent over so I could hear better, looking for his face. "I could get into trouble..." When our eyes met, my anger and frustration took over. Those fucking generals. All those men dead. My Aunt sick and her children helpless...

The adrenaline was wearing off. The camp was on high alert. Everybody was keyed up. I could feel it. People all excited and doin' stuff they wouldn't ordinarily do. It was now or never.

Kurkowski reached through the hole and grabbed my arm. I didn't resist.

"We're just over the hill here, crouch down." Kurkowski half pushed, half carried me across the gravel and over the berm that separated our encampment from the only road in town. The search lights swept the shoreline, but didn't reach us. People were dodging up and down the road. Parked on the shoulder, a dark sedan sat, headlights off, motor running.

The rear door opened and Kurkowski pushed me in. I landed spread-eagled on the back seat and a blanket settled over me as the car lurched into gear and moved onto the road. It was warm and cozy.

Shanghaied

I FELT LIKE I WAS BACK on that freighter that took us to England. I lay with my eyes closed. My nostrils filled with the smell of diesel exhaust and my body rocked with each swell's rise and dip. But this was different.

I pieced together the events that led me here. I remember walking guard duty. The signal flare. Then the shaking fence, a car, a blanket over my head.

Everyone was in a hurry. I was pulled out of the car and spirited up a gangway. Even with the blanket still over my head, I got a whiff of sea air. I was pushed down a corridor, a ladder and another corridor. Then the bang of a metal door, and I was on my own in a tiny cabin.

Eyes opened, I watched a shaft of dim sunlight coming through a porthole as it tracked its way across the floor.

Getting out of the rack revealed a whole new level of mysteries. There were other racks in the room, but they were empty, all made up, nice and tidy. My uniform and rifle were gone. All I had on were my socks and skivvies. Outside the room, voices were chattering away, in some language I couldn't identify, Finnish or Swedish maybe.

I stuck my head out the door and looked up and down an empty passageway. "Hey!" I hollered. "What's goin' on?" One direction led to an open door where the voices were coming from. I could see blue sky. A head appeared.

It was Kurkowski.

"Zewiski." His face broke into his toothy grin. "You finally up?"

"Where the fuck am I and where are my

clothes?" I shed my modesty and marched down the passageway, a chilly breeze in my face, and other places, too. Kurkowski filled the passageway door and met me half way, a blanket in one hand.

"You're late for breakfast," he said, wrapping the blanket over my shoulders, "and inappropriately dressed, I might add."

"I'm shanghaied, is what I am." I tugged the blanket tight and squeezed around the big lug, heading for the open door. "Where you taking me?"

A bright sun and a splash of salt air greeted me when I got out on deck. Water stretched out to the horizon, no land in sight. Three sailor-types, no uniform, offered a good morning in whatever language.

"Don't tell me we're going to Poland because that's just stupid," I muttered while scanning the horizon. Kurkowski laughed.

After translation, the sailors joined in.

"I have some clothes for you in the hold," Kurkowski added after the merriment died down. "Follow me."

I didn't move. "First, tell me what's going on. I demand–"

Kurkowski's smile shriveled. "First clothes, then breakfast, then explanation. Everything in good time." He turned and headed back down the passageway.

There was no point in arguing while I stood exposed to the elements in my skivvies. As I followed Kurkowski, I looked up and saw men staring at me from the bridge.

My clothing allowance consisted of pair of heavy-grade cargo trousers, wool shirt, knit cap and boots. "Keep the blanket," Kurkowski added while I got myself dressed. "It can come in handy."

I wrapped the blanket over my shoulder and

followed Kurkowski up a stairwell to an open doorway that led into a large room.

The ship's common area, a mess hall of sorts, smelled of fried potatoes and onions and fish. A cloud of steam fogged the windows. A large table with benches filled the center of the room. Five people, three men and two women, sat at the table reading newspapers and smoking. Their breakfast plates were scraped clean, but two of the men were still drinking coffee.

Nobody looked up when Kurkowski and I entered. "Get some food and take a seat," he said, pointing at a food service area where a cook was chopping heads of cabbage with a large cleaver. A metal tray with the remains of breakfast sat in front of a mound of potatoes. "I'll be right back."

"Good morning," I said to nobody in particular as I took a space at the table, breakfast plate in one hand, coffee in the other. "Looks to be a lovely day."

The ladies glanced at me and returned tight-lipped smiles. The men ignored me.

I was about to get irritated at their bad manners when one of the men, sitting across from me, lowered his newspaper and nodded. "You must be the American."

"I am American." I replied while I took a cautious sip of the coffee. It was excellent, best I'd ever had. "Do you mean to say I'm the only one?"

The paper he was reading was Polish. "That is correct. You're something of a curiosity. We don't see Americans much these days."

The fried eggs, bread roll and smoked salmon breakfast was cold, but edible. I chewed on a fork-full for a minute and gazed around the table. Except for the man across from me, everyone appeared engrossed in their newspapers. I doubted their sincerity, but I smiled at the man. "I'm curious. Have we been at sea for very long?"

"We land at Lübeck tonight."

I dropped my fork. "Lübeck? Germany?"

The noise got people's attention and newspapers dropped, exposing inquisitive looks.

Panic welled up my throat. I had visions of a squad of Gestapo storm troopers running up the gangway and leading me off to an interrogation room. "What kind of a ship is this!" I stammered. As I pushed my plate away and struggled with the bench to get to my feet, the doorway opened and in stepped Kurkowski carrying a briefcase.

"No need to get up. I hope your breakfast was satisfactory," he said. "Sorry if it was cold."

Eyes wide, I pushed the bench back and gave myself room for battle. These fucking Kraut sympathizers weren't going to take me without a fight. Even if the odds were hopeless.

"Please sit down," Kurkowski said. "It's time for the explaining part."

"I'll say!" I protested. I looked at my seat-mate and back at Kurkowski. "What prison camp are you taking me to?"

Kurkowski gave the man a sour look. "Speaking out of turn, Alfons?"

Alfons grunted and lifted his newspaper in front of his face. "I didn't know," he said behind the Polish News.

"My explanation is not especially rosy, but it's not as bad as you think," Kurkowski said. He took a seat at the head of the table and opened his briefcase. The spring-loaded latches made two loud clicks. "Please," he gestured for me to sit down.

Resistance was futile, for the moment anyway, so I did what I was told. I clutched my coffee mug with both hands to control the shaking and slurped. The rest of the table stared at Kurkowski in rapt attention.

"Let me take a minute to go over the mission agenda for Mister Zewiski's benefit." Kurkowski pulled a portfolio out of the briefcase. He gave me a condescending look and addressed the group. "We are traveling under a Finnish flag. As such, we are accorded all the rights and privileges the German government extends to its allies. Our captain is responsible for our safe passage to Lübeck along with his cargo of contraband products intended for the German Army's high command."

Kurkowski paused and looked at me. "Things like cigarettes and cigars, fine wines and spirits, coffee, luxury apparel and other such items which Germany is in short supply."

I shook my head. "Great, but what about–"

Kurkowski held up a finger to cut me off. "All of us have important duties to carry out for the benefit and preservation of our homeland. And to that end, to guarantee our safety, our travel documents identify us as Polish traitors, working for the German government as translators and informants. Once we disembark from Lübeck we are to proceed to Berlin, via Hamburg, and then to the Polish frontier."

Heads nodded. I started to sweat. I'm an American deserter and now a newly minted Polish traitor traveling to Germany's capital, crawling with Krauts. What next? The River Styx?

I raised my hand. "But what about–"

Kurkowski smiled. "I'll get to you in a minute, Zewiski." He opened the portfolio and studied a paper. "I have just received a message from The

Resistance." He gave everyone but me a stern look. "Listen closely. In Berlin we will be de-briefed by a government official, Herr Fischer, who is sympathetic to our cause. He will provide us with passes to proceed East." Kurkowski made a pregnant pause. "However, Herr Fischer informs us that he cannot guarantee safe passage beyond Berlin."

There was some low murmurs from the quiet folks around the table. One of the two women closed her eyes and sighed. The other took her hand. I wondered what they were going to do in Poland. Nurses? Machine gunners? Cabaret girls? I knew women played many roles in war, just as many as the men and just as dangerous, miserable and thankless.

Kurkowski continued. "This is due to the unstable circumstances now occurring along Germany's Eastern Front. Our comrades with the Polish Resistance will intervene whenever possible, but we cannot depend on their support."

Alfons coughed and cleared his throat. "How will we get through to Polish safe havens?" He looked at me. "Is that why Mister Zewiski is here?"

Not bloody likely. Flabbergasted at the very idea I could be of any assistance getting a crowd of Polish Nationalists across war-torn Eastern Germany, all I could do was give Alfons a blank look, shrug my shoulders and shake my head.

Alfons stared at me, eyebrows raised, like I was a big disappointment.

After another quiet moment studying the paper, Kurkowski took a deep breath and lit a cigarette. "Mister Zewiski will not be accompanying us."

"What?" I didn't know whether to cheer or cry. Since I woke up my world had been a perpetual stress test. I was stumbling around in a pitch-black room full of rattlesnakes and landmines. I slammed my palm against the table. "Now will you tell me what's happening?"

After another drag on his cigarette, Kurkowski gave me a nod. "The Resistance plans to rendezvous with this ship during its return leg to Helsinki. You will be transferred and proceed from there to Danzig."

"Danzig? I don't know anybody in Danzig. My family's in Warsaw."

"Kurkowski sighed. "I am not privy to these matters, Johnny. Apparently, The Resistance wishes to employ your skills and talents at that location. Don't ask me why."

More low-level grousing around the table, some in Polish some in English, me included.

What on earth could The Resistance want with me? I took another sip of my cold coffee. Still good. "If I'm not going with you, then–"

"That's another thing." Kurkowski interrupted me and his sullen expression worsened. "While the ship off-loads at the docks in Lübeck, you obviously pose a threat to our mission's success. Hiding is not a safe option. If the Germans have any suspicion there is a stowaway they will find you. Better to hide you in plain sight. Therefore, the ship's surgeon will render you unconscious, isolate you in quarantine and apply a disguise to give you the appearance of being in the advanced stages of smallpox."

I slumped in my chair and let out a low whistle. One of the women crossed herself. "Pretend I have smallpox? How in the world..." I looked at Kurkowski, "What if the Krauts decide to toss me overboard?"

"There's always a chance they might enforce some on-shore infectious disease contamination ordance," Kurkowski replied. "The captain has your forged Finnish passport and falsified records of your employment onboard this ship. If we're lucky, by international law, that should protect you from being taken into custody by Lübeck's port authorities."

I felt like a gold fish in a toilet, wondering how I got there and worrying about what would happen next.

The ship's horn gave off a loud blast.

"We need to prepare for our departure," Kurkowski said, getting up from the table and stuffing the portfolio back into his briefcase. "We arrive in Lübeck in two hours."

I got a few glances as the others shuffled out, some sympathetic, some not so. Kurkowski motioned me to stay and I waited until we were alone. While the cook peeled potatoes behind the food counter, Kurkowski approached me and held out his hand. This time I took it.

"I wish we could have spent more time together," Kurkowski said. The wrinkles around his blue eyes wavered. "You're a good chap."

"Good chap," I snorted. "You abducted me, stowed me away on a Finnish freighter, now you're turning me over to some blood-thirsty Polish hell-cats and you have the nerve to call me a good chap?"

We both smiled.

"Once this war's over and I recover from my smallpox, I'm gonna look you up so's I can get even," I said.

Kurkowski nodded and headed for the door. "Anything's possible, Johnny."

Numbers, My Good Man

THIS TIME WHEN I OPENED MY EYES I knew I had died and gone to hell. My head hurt like sixty. I was boiling hot and dying of thirst. Every inch of my body was either numb or screaming in pain. And I was tied up. When I tried to move, straps restrained me, buckled tight against my chest and stomach and legs.

"Somebody!" I croaked. "Help!" My tongue would allow only single words and each one took an agonizing effort.

I was in the same room where I woke up the first time. A bleak, depressing metal-gray box with a light in the ceiling and a porthole in one wall. No decorator colors, no cheery, nautical-themed curtains. I would have enjoyed anything to break up the monotony. A calendar from Moe's auto shop in Allentown would be nice. My brothers and I loved to stop in once a month and view the next buxom bombshell who was going to lead us into temptation.

Poor Miss April always took a beating on account of April Fool's day. Every year she'd wind up with the face of a monkey, or the body of a chicken, or whatever, depending on her pose. Last year, Theo stole a picture of my girlfriend, Rosie, and got Moe to paste her face over Miss April's. I got so mad when I saw it I almost stomped out of the shop. When I told Rosie about it, though, she laughed. She said it was an hilarious prank and she hoped the guys enjoyed her company. She could be funny that way sometimes.

The ship was rolling more than before. Sideways and front-to-back. Not a good sign.

I don't remember much about the smallpox caper. When we approached Lübeck, the surgeon tied me on a rack and gave me an injection. He said something like 'don't move' in Finnish-English and that was it.

I guess the ruse didn't work, because it appeared

the Germans have taken over the ship and were letting me die a slow and painful death for my trouble.

"Anybody?" I pleaded to the closed door and empty walls. The ceiling light hurt my eyes so I kept them closed and tried to think good thoughts.

A screeching sound of metal against metal interrupted my concentration. Great. We've hit an iceberg and the ship's breaking apart. Good timing. Now add copious amounts of cold Baltic Sea water to my misery. At least that would cool down my fever.

A cool cloth settled over my eyes and forehead.

"Be easy," someone said. The smell of fried herring came along with the command.

I opened my mouth. "Waaater."

Precious drops landed on the extended wasteland that was my tongue. "More," I mumbled.

Torture. This had to be some kind of German torture. Very effective.

There was so much I wanted to say, to confess, whatever, but all that came out was, "More."

My request started a barrage of words in that Finnish-sounding language. It definitely was not German. The words came from two sources. I wasn't included in the conversation.

"Open," somebody said in my direction. I obliged, assuming they meant mouth.

More water trickled on my tongue. Then another needle prick in my arm and the world went black again.

The ship was still rolling when I woke up the next time, but I felt better. Someone jostled my shoulder. I looked into a face, reeking of fried herring and blocking the ceiling light.

The face broke into a smile and moved back a few inches, much to my relief.

"Better now?"

I grunted and tried not to appear too enthusiastic.

"Gutt," the face said, followed by "Up."

Ten wobbly paces later, I was ushered to a toilet, then a sink.

I'm not much on personal hygiene. A couple years slogging across North Africa and Sicily introduced some bad habits that blotted out everything Mama had taught me. Toilet paper was a scarcity so we had to improvise. Tooth brush? wash cloth? wash behind the ears? Fuhgetaboutit. But a splash of water did much to clear the cobwebs, as Mama used to say.

With a clean face and outfitted in fresh clothes, I leaned heavily against a stout sailor as he escorted me upstairs to the same mess hall where I had been briefed by Kurkowski.

It was rough going as the ship continued to rock and roll. Our brief turn-around outside between decks was greeted with howling winds and salt spray. It was still daylight, but barely. Dark clouds scudded above the horizon between a setting sun and the white-capped sea. Overhead, a crescent moon blinked in between the clouds.

The mess hall still smelled of fried potatoes, fish and onions.

"Good evening, Mister Zewiski," a commanding-looking blond fellow in a blue and white turtle-neck sweater got up from one of the tables and assisted me to a bench. "Welcome aboard the *Alholmen*." He waved my walking companion off and returned to his seat. "May I get you a cup of coffee?"

I nodded, remembering my last cup was the best I ever had.

"Sorry, but no food for a little while," he added,

while setting my half-full coffee mug on the pitching table.

I held on with both hands and took a careful first sip. Excellent.

"Your stomach hasn't fully recovered yet."

"Recovered? From what?"

I eyed the fellow. He had a thick, bushy beard and was wearing a cap with a distinctive brim. No scrambled eggs, but it looked like something an officer would wear.

"From your pretend bout of smallpox. We had to make you look pretty bad. Fortunately, the Germans were convinced."

I took another sip of coffee. The aroma and flavor almost put me in a swoon. "You certainly convinced me," I said. "Where do you get this coffee?"

"Hawaii. Kona coffee. The best in the world. We make the Germans pay for it in gold bullion, which they pay gladly."

The image of topless ladies wearing grass skirts and dancing the hula hula appeared in my mind. I remembered the look on Al's face when Theo told us about Hawaii. The radio announcer was talking about bombs, and then I was running through traffic, toward the recruitment center...

When I noticed the guy was waiting, I blurted out, "Are you the captain?"

"At your service, Mister Zewiski." He reached over and we shook hands. Karvonen, Ernesti Karvonen. Call me Earnest."

The ship took a profound shudder and the lights flickered.

Earnest twisted in his seat and glanced at a sailor stationed by the door. They had some sort of silent conversation then Earnest turned back around to me. "We're entering a patch of rough weather. For us, as you would say in America, it's good news and bad news."

"How could it be anything but bad news?" I said.

Earnest's smile trailed off to a tight-lipped grimace and he hunched over the table. He stared into his coffee mug for a minute, then looked into my eyes, a serious look.

"I was told Mister Kurkowski explained to you the arrangement to hand you over to the Polish resistance while on our return voyage to Finland."

I nodded and took another long sip of magic Kona coffee. A glimmer of dread fidgeted in the back of my head.

"Well, we convinced the Germans you had the smallpox, but they were suspicious, as always."

Another shudder passed through the ship. Not as bad as the last one.

"They've been monitoring us since we left Lübeck, which makes the hand-off difficult. The Poles are in position, but once we make any heading or speed change the Germans will pursue us. They would love nothing more than to uncover our hand-off plan and, legitimately, under international law, confiscate their money and probably sink us."

I watched Earnest's jaw clench.

I spoke up to avoid hearing bad news. "So you've called off the arrangement?"

He blinked and sat straight in his chair. "At first, it seemed that we would, but now that we have this storm, we still have a chance."

I took a deep breath. My dread took on substance as I read Earnest's mind. "The storm hides you from the Krauts?"

"Exactly."

"But..."

"Yes." Earnest got up from his chair, walked to the door and looked out the porthole.

It was dark now. I don't know what he saw, but he came back in a hurry and avoided me while I waited for an answer.

"The hand-off is more difficult, but not impossible." He dropped his mug in the dirty dish sink. "You'll have to excuse me, Mister Zewiski. I need to return to the bridge. My first mate, Heimo, will fill you in with the details."

Heimo's English was third-grade level, but he didn't have to say much. It was a simple plan. They were going to wrap me in thermal underwear, buckle a helmet on my head, strap me in five Mae Wests, from neck to knees, then attach me to a rope and, using a crane, suspend me over the water near the Polish ship. He chuckled when he said he hoped the Poles had a *pole*, haha, long enough to snag the rope and reel me in.

I, being the one hanging at the end of the rope, didn't see much humor in his clever double entendre. All this was to take place in the dark of night in a howling gale. An hour from now.

Right. He explained it like it was no problem at all. It was such a stupid idea I didn't bother to complain. But I still couldn't fathom why the Finns and Polacks were going to all this trouble for a stupid GI private, recently turned deserter, who wanted to save his Aunt and her two children. I didn't have a shred of credibility, I didn't even have a security clearance. My biggest Army claim to fame was shaking that weasel Patton's hand in Sicily after we took Troina.

"Why me?" I said to Heimo.

"The invasion, you know about this," he replied.

"Invasion? What invasion?"

"From England. Where you came from."

"Heimo, I don't know what the hell you're talking about. I was in Slapton, sure. But there wasn't any invasion going on."

Heimo smiled. "OK," he said. "Let's go."

With a firm hand under my armpit, he escorted me back to my sleeping quarters and dressed me for the ordeal to come.

It was while I hung suspended over the raging Baltic Sea that it dawned on me. Claptown. The training exercises with the Brits. They thought it was training for an Allied invasion. Holy shit! Were they in for a disappointment.

It took three tries for the Polacks to snag me. Dangling like a sack of potatoes, twisting in the wind, I watched helplessly while two gigantic ships struggled against the storm not to smash into each other with me in the middle. The wind and spray made it hard to see, but the noise scared the hell out of me. Churning engines and frantic shouts from both sides, in Finnish and Polish. The extended crane accentuated the *Alholmen*'s pitch and I swayed in wild, long arcs over the dark water. Talk about a moving target. I worried at any minute both sides were going to give up, drop me in the drink and go their merry ways.

Twice the Polacks closed in only to be smacked by an unexpected wave, lurching them off their course and requiring a complete turn-around and realignment. I had a feeling the third attempt was the go/no-go occurrence.

I heard a faint Huzzah when the line above my head jerked toward the Polack ship, but I was so disoriented, soaked and freezing cold, I couldn't tell from where it came. It didn't matter because the next instant my worst fears were realized. I dropped into the Baltic and was dragged under water like a hooked flounder.

Heimo didn't say anything about being dropped into the sea. Was this part of the plan? I wondered while I banged against the Polish boat's hull. Or had something gone dreadfully wrong. Again.

While my lungs screamed for air, a scene about keel-hauling flashed in my troubled mind. It was from 'Mutiny on the Bounty' I had read in Miss Huckaby's English class. Little did I know then, that I would experience the sensation first hand.

At least, unlike Captain Bligh's victims, the Mae Wests acted like protective bumpers while I bounced against a hard steel hull.

The Polacks reeled me in and ignominiously pitched me onto the deck as the vague silhouette of the *Alholmen* churned away into inky darkness.

Several hands unfastened my tether and removed the Mae Wests while I coughed up sea water. Once freed, they carried me through a door into a warmer place. In a tiny, airless room I changed out of my soaking wet Finnish clothes into dry Polish clothes. Another new identity. I was having a hard time keeping track of who I was.

"Witamy," a seaman in black fatigues said, once I was dry. No smiles this time. The cramped space smelled of stale tobacco and mold.

"Cheers," I waved back, assuming he had given me a greeting.

He handed me a tin cup of dark, hot liquid. It tasted terrible, but at least it was hot. I missed my Kona coffee.

I looked at the sailor's dour face and sighed.

Here we go again. Another bouncy ship, another strange language, more bad news. I was confident about the bad news part.

I got another command in Polish and the sailor pointed down a hallway. I recognized the word Kapitan. The tin cup swayed with the ship while I gagged my way through another sip of the dark, liquid crap.

"Sure, why not?" In my present state of mind, I couldn't wait to give the guy the bad news about their invasion.

I was led to another odoriferous room crammed with radio equipment. One fellow sat in front of the radios, his ears covered with enormous headphones. Another fellow stood next to him holding a clipboard. My escort pointed at a stool under a small table covered with charts and navigation instruments.

"Siedzieć," he said, pointing at a chair.

Like a good puppy, I did what I was told.

Underneath a static noise, the headphone guy was jabbering away in German while the guy with the clipboard took furious notes.

Suddenly, the guy with the clipboard jumped to the door and stuck his head out. He shouted something urgent. It sounded like 'Utknac' or whatever.

Then everything went quiet. I mean everything. The ship's motors stopped, all the lights went out, nobody moved. The three men put on helmets. I was left unprotected.

"Hey!" I yelled at clipboard. "What am I, chopped liver?" My complaint was smothered by a BOOM, another BOOM, followed by a tremendous roar, like that made by an airplane passing overhead, six inches overhead.

I ducked under the table. It sounded like the

Krauts were on to us and we were all chopped liver.

The guy with the clipboard shouted out the door again, poleciec! or something. The ship immediately came back to life and we took off like a bat out of hell.

I rubbed my neck after the whiplash sensation, and while we flew over the Baltic's troubled waters, I ventured a question. "What was that?"

"A Junkers '87," clipboard replied.

The English caught me off-guard. "And? Is he coming back?"

No answer besides German babble over the radios.

I raised my voice over the babble. "Will you tell me what's going on?"

Clipboard turned away from the radios and noticed me for the first time. "It's a game of ducks and drakes, old chap." His English was the King's kind. "Or cat and mouse, as you Yanks would put it."

"Ducks and what?"

"Pleased to meet you, Mister Zewiski, Clifton Barns, here. Call me Cliff."

"Likewise, Cliff. What's goin' on?"

I clutched the anchored table while the ship careened over waves. Cliff seemed to be used to rough sailing. He effortlessly compensated for the ups and downs, bending his knees and swaying back and forth.

He patted the radio guy on the shoulder and took a step in my direction. Now that the excitement was over, Cliff seemed eager to talk.

"You see, old chap, we're in touch with the German coastal authorities, pretending to be one of their shore patrol boats. We were following a pre-planned route, ostensibly tailing that Finnish trawler, but when we stopped for fifteen minutes and then proceeded without comment, the Germans went from suspicious to hostile. They hailed us to change frequency, use a different code set and come to a dead stop, all in a matter of three minutes. The Junkers then made a pass and dropped two fifty-kilogram bombs at the point where we would have been if we had not followed directions."

"Jesus Christ," I muttered. "Why haven't you clever people won the war?"

Cliff smiled. "Numbers, my good man, a mere matter of numbers. And, I'm told, that's where you come in."

"About that very thing." I sat up straight and cleared my throat. "Sorry to tell you, but I don't–"

Cliff held up a hand, pursed his lips and shook his head. "Not another word, please, Mister Zewiski."

"But one of the Finnish sailors, he said something about–"

"PLEASE!" Cliff nearly pounced on me. "I said not another word and I mean it. The less I know the better. Speaking selfishly, I have a low tolerance for pain. If I knew anything and if the Germans got their hands on me I'd sing like a canary. Understand?"

I gave Cliff a contrite nod and wondered about *my* fate.

After an awkward minute, Cliff smiled again. "Awfully sorry for the drama, old chap, but save your comments for Danzig. We'll be there soon."

Danzig

THE EASTERN HORIZON TURNED FROM BLACK to a dark blue haze punctuated by stands of trees and untamed vegetation.

"Where's Danzig?" I looked at the helmsman, but he didn't look up from the view window. Probably because he had his hands full, steering the ship at a dangerously high rate of speed, weaving in and out of sandbars and snags, just yards from a ragged white line I figured were waves breaking against the shore.

I expected to see a city, at least the outskirts of one. Everyone was always saying Danzig this and Danzig that. The free city, whatever that meant. All it had to show for itself was a deserted shoreline. Not a building in sight.

Cliff, crouched next to the helmsman, mumbled instructions in Polish. He looked up at me in the dim cabin light and winked. "It's behind that tree line. Welcome to German-occupied Poland. Enter at your own risk."

Muzzle flashes lit up from the trees. Tracers whined overhead and we took a few hits, but not enough to stop us. I guess it wasn't deserted.

"I suppose we've worn out our welcome," Cliff said.

The static and German babble coming from the radio room went dead just as the ship made a neck-snapping right turn and entered a narrow estuary. It was light enough now that I could make out a forest of tall rushes lining both sides of the waterway.

Cliff stood and pointed at a mass of shrubbery.

The helmsman turned again, left this time, into a green wall.

I braced myself against the bulkhead as we plowed through, waiting for impact. A last ditch, suicide maneuver? I was too tense to ask.

The ship shuddered to a stop. Cliff opened the cabin door and looked outside. "This way. Quick."

He disappeared by the time I was out the door. I followed the path of broken reeds that revealed his passage. The pop-pop sound of small arms fire followed me.

A gloved hand pressed against my chest, blocking my way. "Cliff?" I peered into the reeds.

A large figure stood motionless. It wasn't Cliff.

The figure said something that sounded like 'sledzic' and some other words.

I stared at the guy and hesitated. "Who the hell–?"

A violent push from behind sent me sprawling, my face buried in oozy vegetable matter. I lay still. It was time to concede defeat. The Germans had us. It was a suicide mission after all. I hoped they wouldn't torture poor Cliff. I'd be happy to tell them everything they wanted to know.

Voices above me spoke in rapid Polish. I recognized one of them as Cliff.

"Hummmpf," I sputtered.

I struggled to lift my face free from the mud when two pair of hands, one on each side, grabbed me by the arm pits and jerked me forward.

The only noise was the sound of boots treading through deep muck. My capturers were moving too fast for me to get my footing, so I let them drag me through the bullrushes of northern Poland, right under the noses of a ruthless German occupying army. Was this trainwreck ever going to end?

I kept my head down to avoid getting my face slapped by vegetation until we reached a clearing. We stopped at the perimeter and I was lifted to my feet. Around me, three men stood motionless, not saying anything.

A flash of reflected sunlight appeared on the opposite side of the clearing. We sprinted across and rushed through an opened camouflaged trap door and down a flight of stairs into a dark well.

"Mister Zewiski, please take a seat." My companions dropped me into a rickety wooden chair and disappeared into the shadows. The chair sank as the floor planks settled in the muddy ground.

A man in camouflage fatigues and a black beret sat next to a small table in front of me, smoking a cigarette. Illuminated by a single candle, he had a thin mustache and small, piercing eyes that bored a hole right through me.

We were in a dug-out cave. Water dripped from the wooden-braced ceiling, along the walls and pooled on the floor's rough-hewn planks. The air was damp and close, almost suffocating. It was familiar.

We used to dig cave forts in Allentown. We would dig them under the road so we could feel cars' vibrations as they rolled by overhead, oblivious, of course, to the danger of a cave-in. We'd bring down candles and candy, a cigarette and whatever forbidden contraband we could get our hands on. Great fun. The caves always collapsed during a hard rain. Theo made sure the cave's entrance had at least one tight, narrow turn to enhance my claustrophobia.

The man held up a package of cigarettes I didn't recognize and offered me a smoke. I scrunched my nose and shook my head.

"I don't blame you." The man spoke very good English, the American kind. "Life is too short for cigarettes made from granulated wood byproducts." He looked at the cigarette and smiled. "Still, it's the thought that counts. Don't you agree?"

I blinked at him and ignored his superficial question. I'd gone through too much to waste time with small talk. "Do you want to find out about an invasion?"

He didn't answer. Instead, he barked something

in Polish and a minute later a bottle of clear liquid appeared along with two shot glasses.

"Yes," the man said as he poured, "but first, let me offer you an ounce, as you Americans would say, of Polish hospitality. There'll be time enough for invasion talk."

I'm not a vodka drinker, but a taste of the real thing was tempting. The liquid shimmered in the candle light, its surface, ruffled by some unknown vibrations, reminded me of boyhood root beer parties in our cave forts. It'd probably kick like a mule, but why not? When in Poland...

"To Poland," he said.

"To Poland," I replied and joined him as he raised his glass and gulped.

It burned going down, but otherwise I didn't feel a thing.

Three shots later, I was too drunk to move. It was hard to stay in my seat because the room was spinning. My eyelids were heavy and getting heavier. The man sitting across the table was talking, in English, I think. He jabbered away, but I didn't have any idea what he was saying.

"It's been a long day," I slurred as I slid off the chair. "Mind if I lie down?"

I didn't want to disappoint the Polish Resistance Fighters. Hell, I had nobody else to turn to, but I had a sinking feeling they weren't going to be happy with me.

The smell of frying onions interfered with a dream I was having. Rosie and I were driving through the countryside, outside Allentown. The windows were down and the wind ruffled Rosie's hair. We were going for a picnic, but the fried onions made no sense...

When I opened my eyes, the man with the thin mustache was still sitting, staring at me. I felt clammy from lying on the wet planks. Now, the fried onions made me hungry.

Once I climbed back in my seat, he talked like nothing had happened since the vodka. "You have family in Warsaw. An Aunt and her two children. Yes?"

"That's right." I looked for the onions. "Bazyli, her husband, died fighting the Germans," I added.

The man nodded. "I am sorry for your loss. I also have family in Warsaw. My wife is there, along with her parents. She wouldn't join me when an escape was possible because her parents were not capable of withstanding the rigors that were involved." He reached in his pocket and pulled out a package of cigarettes, the same ones as before. He looked at me, saw the scowl on my face, and put them back. "Are your parents alive?"

"Yes," I replied. "They live in Pennsylvania, where I grew up."

A pitcher and two glasses appeared, along with a plate of onions and potatoes. The man looked at me and winked. "Water this time," he said. "Polish water is as good as its Vodka."

I poured myself a glass and dived into the food while he kept talking. "I have heard of Pennsylvania. It must be a beautiful place. The birthplace of your nation, correct?"

"Yeah, that's what it says in the history books. I don't know much about all that."

The man stared at his empty glass. "Can I help you, Mister Zewicki? I understand you want to rescue your family in Warsaw. Is that right?"

I nodded.

"Do you have something in mind? A plan, perhaps?"

"I wanted to be a part of an Allied engagement to end the German occupation. That's what I signed up for, and what they promised, but it didn't happen. So I left. The Resistance helped me... Helped me escape." I fidgeted in my seat thinking about desertion. "I don't know what I can do, all by myself. I'm just following my nose, I guess."

"Maybe there is something, Mister Zewiski."

I finished my water and burped. The potatoes were delicious. "Do you have a name?" I cocked my head and gave him a quizzical look.

"No," he replied. "If the Germans find out you have spoken to a member of the Polish Resistance you will merely get shot. Knowing a name, even a false one, will result in hours of torture until the absence of death becomes a torture unto itself."

He shifted in his seat. "It's better if you have no knowledge of my name. Bad enough to be having this conversation."

I cleared my throat. "About our conversation. Like I said, if you're asking about an Allied invasion, I've got news for you. It ain't gonna happen."

There was a long pause and the man leaned back in his chair. By the strained look on his face, I could tell he wanted another cigarette bad.

"But the training. You were a participant in training exercises. How do you mean, it ain't gonna happen?"

"The training turned into a disaster. One day we were supposed to have a live-fire exercise, no big deal, bullets over our heads. But instead, things got mixed up, some of the LSTs weren't where they were supposed to be, and when we marched ashore, we came under fire. A lot of guys were killed. A real bad situation."

"But we never heard of such a situation."

I glared at the guy, remembering the horror of that morning. "That's because the mother-fucking generals ordered us to keep it a secret."

The man's face turned pale. He fidgeted with the pitcher. "Really?"

It was the first time the guy said an impromptu word. "Yeah," I continued. "Then to top it off, the next day some Kraut submarines attacked. They sunk six LSTs and a whole lot more men died. Hundreds."

The man got up out of his chair and shouted up the stairs in Polish, fast and loud.

When he turned back toward me, he had a pale, anxious look on his face. "What is your assessment about the outcome of this calamity?"

"Well, if there was a plan to invade Germany, it ain't happening now. Not after what I saw. The whole beach was on fire, a regular shit-storm. Sinking ships, men dying in burning oil. The Krauts are on to the deal. There's no surprise. It's over."

He sat in his chair and stared at the ceiling. "All along, our British agents have assured us the Allied invasion will take place, but they didn't know when or where. Sometime in June or July was all they could tell us. The success of our uprising, starting in Warsaw, depends on the Allies opening a second front to the West. We hoped you could confirm the invasion so we could coordinate a counterattack. Instead, you say it's not happening?"

"If it does, the whole fucking western arm of the German army is going to be there to greet them. I'm telling ya."

Voices from outside came down from above.

The man nodded. He took off his beret and ran his fingers through his hair. "We need to verify. Do you have any contacts?"

"Talk to Kurkowski, The guy was on to everything, I'm sure–"

"Dead, I'm afraid." He poured himself some water. "The Polish sympathizer in Berlin was a double cross. They were all executed."

I slunk down and let out a long breath. "That's too bad. Then I can't help you. Even if I knew somebody, my current status as a deserter won't open many doors."

We stared at each other in silence. Each in our own thoughts.

"Tell me the names of the American and British high command who were associated with the invasion plans."

"Well," I thought for a minute. "There was General Eisenhower, 'Ike' they call him. He was the head honcho, along with General Omar Bradley. And the Brits had General Montgomery. My outfit, the First Infantry Division, was led by General Huebner."

The man nodded, got up and gestured for me to follow. "Those names match our intelligence reports. Your story is plausible enough that it is worth the risk of a sortie."

He shouted some more orders.

"Wait a minute. What are you talking about?" I slowly got up. I understood one of his Polish words, 'latać.' It meant flee or run; something like that. "What's a sortie?"

"A courier flight. Our commander in Warsaw must hear your story in person before we make contingency plans. You will be transported to Warsaw," he said as we climbed the stairs.

My jaw dropped and I stopped at the bottom of the access ladder. "Are you nuts? Fly over occupied Poland? Crowded with German Luftwaffe?"

The man stopped for a moment. "Don't worry, my friend."

When we reached the surface, he walked toward a low building. An array of camouflaged antennas jutted out from the building's roof line. "It's only three-hundred kilometers from here. We have good pilots. It's not quite a suicide mission."

When he got to the door, he turned around. "And don't forget, Mister Zewiski, you'll get your wish. You'll meet your family!"

Turned out it was a suicide mission, for the pilot.

The kill shot took off part of one wing. The one on my side.

Our plane went down in a hail of anti-aircraft fire right when the pilot pointed at a dull, reddish-yellow glow in the black void ahead of us. "Warsaw," he said. It looked like a sunrise in hell.

We were hedge-hopping, seemingly undetected until we woke up some Krauts manning a perimeter defense installation, heretofore unknown by the Polish Resistance. The plane flipped over, followed by a few seconds of free-fall then crashing noises; branches exploding around us, then a jolting stop.

Upside down, I struggled with the seat harness when I heard a bubbling noise. A window strut stuck out of my pilot's chest. "Go," he said. "You have three minutes only."

It was pitch black. No fire.

After I dropped out of the cockpit, it was eerily quiet for a moment until I made my first step, which sounded like a twenty-piece marching band. Other steps, along with lights, shouts in German and barking joined in, heading in my direction.

Twenty hasty and loud paces later, the plane blew up in a tremendous ball of flame. The shock wave threw me to the ground and covered me with smoldering leaves and branches. I suppose the Resistance fighters had it booby-trapped for just such an occurrence. Not quite a suicide mission, the man with the thin mustache had said. Ha.

The German shouts turned into screams and cries.

The ensuing fire illuminated a thick stand of trees around me. I craned my neck from my prone position and twisted around, looking for shelter. A hole in the foliage caught my attention. It didn't look like much, but any old port in a storm.

It's amazing how the smallest fragment of shelter can seem impenetrable to a desperate man. Hiding behind a stick, a branch, and your imagination makes you feel like you've disappeared. Nobody will find me here, I kept telling myself. Pathetic.

When the path played out and I crashed into a wall of spiny vines, I crawled into the thicket and lay still, taking deep breaths and waited for my heart to slow down. The Poles had given me a side arm and I whispered a prayer of thanks when I felt for the holster and found it still strapped to my waist.

The screaming had stopped.

I hoped the German recovery team would conclude everyone on the plane died in the explosion and go home.

The cover of darkness wasn't going to last long.

The damn trail. It's gotta go somewhere. Now that my eyes were accustomed to the black, I peered into the branches around me, shifting ever so slightly to get a better look. Maybe I missed a turn. Concentrating, straining for any clues, the sound of running water caught my attention. It wasn't a big sound, a little stream maybe, but it promised a passage.

After an hour of low-crawling over a rocky stream bed I slowly stood up, soaking wet. The first rays of sunlight had broken through the dense surroundings. Tree trunks loomed around me. Overhead, I could hear aircraft, but they were hidden behind the canopy. I had been concentrating on survival, one inch at a time, but I couldn't help the occasional sigh of despair. Maybe it was a better idea to give up and negotiate. If I told the Germans there wasn't going to be an invasion they would... They would what? Hand me over to the American Army? Set me free in Warsaw? Damn. It was real easy to wonder what's the point.

That's when Jakub showed up.

"You lost?" he said. The muzzle of his carbine tapped me on the back of my neck and I nearly shit my pants.

Hands up, I turned and faced the stalker. The guy was huge, easily six feet and way over two-hundred pounds. I thought I was quiet. How he snuck up on me I'll never know, but my heart started beating again when he broke into a toothy grin.

"American?"

"How'd you guess?" Even in ripped-up, filthy Polish fatigues I guess I stood out like a sore thumb. Maybe it was my haircut.

"You in that plane that was goin' to Warsaw?" He dropped his weapon when I nodded.

"I'm Jakub. Follow me."

Warsaw

JAKUB LED ME to an abandoned warehouse sitting on the edge of a torn up pasture. "You're very lucky," he said after we got settled. We took up an upstairs corner space that gave us high-angle views in two directions.

The warehouse had been shelled and burned. Both floors were littered with the remains of farm equipment and busted sacks of supplies. The scent of charred wood and god knows what else permeated the interior. Holes in the roof let in rays of sunlight filled with dust.

"They know you got away. You did the right thing following the creek bed, but they'll catch up." Jakub pulled out a flask from inside his fatigue jacket and, while he opened it, he looked out the two openings that used to be windows. "Let's hope your luck holds out until tonight."

Jakub's vodka wasn't as smooth as the drink I had before. It had a bitter, starchy flavor. I took one politeness sip and shook my head the next time around.

"What's the matter," Jakub frowned. "My vodka not good enough for your refined American taste?"

I chuckled and avoided Jakub's stare. "No offense, but I had a bad experience two days ago in Danzig. I still haven't recovered."

Jakub shrugged his shoulders and, after another swallow, put the flask back in his jacket. His eyes never left the windows. "We were told to expect a courier flight from Danzig, nothing else. Seems odd it would include an American. What were you doing in Danzig, besides drinking?"

I sighed and followed his gaze at open, pockmarked pasture land, studded with broken machinery and litter. A dead horse lay near the remains of a wagon, its swollen belly covered with flies. In between the carnage, clusters of irises, poppies and crocuses bloomed in a riot of color. Heaven and hell can sometimes find room for each other.

"It's a long story," I said. "Tell me yours first. Your English is very good. How come?"

"I grew up in Cleveland. You know about Cleveland?" He looked at me and smiled.

I smiled back and rolled my eyes. The tension in my shoulders relaxed. "That explains it. Another volunteer. How long you been here?"

"Years. Since 1939. I'm more Polish than American now."

After a long session of back and forth about Cleveland, Allentown, Claptown, Danzig and Warsaw I learned that Jakub had two brothers. One was in the Navy, somewhere in the South Pacific. The other brother was fifteen. Jakub had left home for Poland for the same reason I did, only he didn't trust the Army to get him there.

"My father hates the military and advised me not to enlist. So I hopped a freighter and made my way to Warsaw just ahead of the Germans." He frowned. "I met up with my relatives, but there was little I could do to help them. It took a long time to gain membership in good standing with the resistance forces. Out of five, only one relation, a cousin, is still alive." Jakub stared at the ceiling. "At this point, I'm not sure who is making a difference, me or my brother."

"I think you made the right decision," I said. "Better than mine."

Jakub handed me a slice of black bread and some cheese. "We'll have to keep watch until nightfall."

"If you'll excuse me," I sighed, leaning back

against an exploded seat cushion. I couldn't keep my eyes open any longer. "Hope you don't mind if I let you take the first watch."

Jakub grunted.

I took one last look out the window next to me. It was past midday. Clouds covered the afternoon sun. The breeze coming in the window felt chilly. And damp.

"Time to go." I heard Jakub's voice inside the dream I kept having about Rosie. We were still in the car heading for the Lehigh river for our picnic, but my brothers were in the back seat. I was shouting at them to shut up. Al was wearing a military uniform. Theo had on a gangster-looking outfit. Just before the dream dissolved, Rosie turned and smiled at me. "Don't be sad, Johnny dear," she said.

"Wait a minute," I sputtered, not sure if I was talking to Jakub or my girlfriend.

"No time to wait," Jakub replied. I could barely see him in what had become a cold, dark space. He was crouched, alternately looking at me and the windows. "They're here," he whispered. "Stay away from the windows."

I shook the cobwebs out of my head and struggled to leave the dream. Focusing on Jakub, I crawled behind him to the top of the stairwell. The floor was slick from rain gusting in through holes in the walls and roof.

Shrill German voices and beams from powerful flashlights came up the stairs from the ground floor.

"They sound tired and cold," Jakub whispered. "Four of them. I can't tell if they're still looking for you or seeking shelter from the rain."

He set his carbine on the floor and removed a long-bladed knife from inside his jacket. It looked like a bayonet from an American M-1 rifle. "Either way, we need to kill them now, before they get their strength back."

I looked at his carbine. "No good in close quarters," he said. He pointed at my holster. "I hope that thing works."

Heavy footsteps came from the bottom of the stairs. "You shoot this one," Jakub said. "Then step aside and let me pass around you. Follow me close."

I'd never killed anyone point-blank before. Plenty of times in Sicily I pointed my rifle and fired at puffs of smoke; made a lot of noise, mostly, but I never saw anyone die by my own hand. That's the advantage of being part of a team. You get bragging rights, most of the time unwarranted, but who knows?

I swallowed hard and wiped my sweaty hand on my pants before pulling the pistol from its holster. "It's me or you, pal," I whispered. My hand shook as I readied myself; pistol out. Jakub switched off the safety for me. Finger on the trigger, I held my shooting hand with my free hand to steady the weaving barrel. This wasn't the time to choke.

Jakub gave me a gentle push. "Move," he whispered.

The Kraut was half-way up the stairs when I sprang into the stairwell and fired. He filled up most of the space. It was an easy shot, but it wasn't. After the noise and smoke, he staggered back, sunk to his knees and clung to the bannister. He was still gasping when I squeezed myself next to him to make room for Jakub. It was an eerie feeling, both frightening and sympathetic, to be so close to a dying man.

My sentiments were interrupted when Jakub kicked him hard in the face on his way down the stairwell, sending him backwards, like a sack of seed, to the bottom of the stairs.

When I got to the downstairs room, one Kraut was lying prone on the floor and Jakub was struggling with the third. Both of them were about the same size and they grappled furiously, twisting and turning. The fourth was approaching them, pistol raised, waiting for a clear shot.

"Achtung!" I shouted in my best German Gruppenführer accent. The fourth Kraut instinctively turned and looked at me. This time I didn't hesitate shooting before he realized I was a fake. I emptied the pistol, sending him to the floor.

My warning also surprised the Kraut grappling with Jakub. He hesitated a fraction of a second, allowing Jakub a chance to free himself from the man's grip and slide his knife deep into the Kraut's chest. Eyes wide, the Kraut looked confused and unhappy as he slumped to his knees and fell face forward on top of his partner.

Jakub grabbed one of the Germans' weapons and leaped back, away from the front door toward the rear of the building. "This way," he gasped. The tone of his voice was high and panicky, so different from our conversation upstairs I hardly recognized it.

I stripped the fourth German's service belt, with holster and ammo pouch, and followed blindly, kicking and shoving my way across the floor strewn with debris and bodies.

Daybreak found us making our way along a low ridge-line a mile or so from a river. Clusters of houses and buildings stood on the other side. The storm had blown off. Scattered clouds dotted the horizon, illuminated by the rising sun. I was still shaken by yesterday's violence and I tried to ease my troubled thoughts about taking a life by appreciating the view.

A breeze came off the river carrying a noxious, acidic stink. It stopped me in my tracks.

"What the devil is that?" I said, gagging on the words.

"Warsaw," came the matter-of-fact reply. "It takes getting used to."

An hour later, we crouched behind a rocky, protected vantage point at the edge of a thick grove of aspens, and looked down on the smoldering city. A gray cloud hung over the shattered skyline. Overhead, a German Stuka bomber circled and dived like a hawk.

"The smell is from destroyed tanneries and chemical plants, decomposing animals, open sewers, you name it."

The thought of my aunt and her children living down there made me wonder how they could possibly survive. "It looks hopeless."

"That's what the Germans want us to believe. 'There's nothing left to defend,' they keep telling us. Motherfuckers. They want us to stop resisting like they're doing us a favor."

I coughed, then took in another lung-full of rancid fumes. "I hate bringing your commander bad news about the invasion, Jakub." I put my hand over my mouth. "But from the looks of things, it probably won't matter much."

Jakub hesitated before answering. "I still don't believe you." He avoided looking at me. "A screw-up the size you describe would be an embarrassment, but not enough of one to cancel a full-scale, coordinated Allied invasion that's been planned for at least a year now."

"All I know is what I saw. Hundreds of men dead and dying on the beach and floating in the flaming water. German submarines shooting torpedoes indiscriminately, no deterrent. It doesn't get much worse than that."

Jakub kept his eyes focussed on Warsaw. Jaw clenched, he turned and gave me a serious stare. "It's a matter of numbers, Johnny. What's a few hundred dead, and a few thousand more when all is said and done, compared to the millions that will most certainly be dead throughout Europe if they don't invade?"

I sat quietly. Cliff had talked about numbers while we dodged bombs in the Baltic Sea. But how, in good conscience, could those generals ask their troops to march into harm's way after screwing up as bad as they did?

"Anyway," Jakub added. They have to do something soon with all those horny, bored and bad-mannered troops before the English shoo them off the island themselves."

"Good point," I said. We both chuckled, but I wondered about Jakub's argument. All I knew is what I saw. But did I fail to see a bigger picture?

"Follow me and stay close," Jakub nodded his head toward the trail we'd been following. It led away from the aspen grove into an open field. Tall grass covered its path leading to the river. He shouldered the German submachine gun and took out his bayonet. "Stay crouched," he said. "And keep your voice down. From here on, land mines and tripwires everywhere. We have to do this stretch in daylight. I'll look down and you look up. Touch me if you see anything."

"Are the mines German?"

"Polish," Jakob replied. "The Resistance set them just before the Germans came to town to protect this trail."

We crept down the trail, crouched below the hedges and grasses, a step at a time. I was reminded of my session crawling in the stream bed last night. Being so close to little things. Beetles and ants and crickets and mice. Bees buzzed around our ears. Starlings swooped over our heads, not noticing us as we lumbered along like a couple of lost turtles, imposing on a Lilliputian world that took no notice of our presence.

My back was killing me and my thighs were screaming.

"There's a farm ahead," Jakub whispered, his face glued to the trail. He must have heard my moaning. "A man will appear at the door. Touch me when you see him."

Straining my legs to look above our green cover hurt even more, but there it was, a house. Damaged, but intact. The front door was closed and I couldn't make out any movement around the premises.

"Get down!" Jakub hissed.

Below the house, a road followed the river. I didn't notice it at first, concentrating on the house, but Jakub heard them coming, or more likely felt them. A convoy. Five German military vehicles including a lorry.

We froze in our tracks, listening and peeking at the road through our paltry cover, hoping the convoy would pass the house, but it stopped.

"Shit," Jakob swore under his breath. He turned, looked back up the trail, then shook his head. "Help me count how many," he said.

An officer got out of the front car. Two solders followed. Three more jumped out the back of the lorry and idled on the road, smoking. Another ran up to the farmhouse front door as the officer entered. Some shouts came from inside the house and the three men on the road trotted toward the rear.

"Looks like four in the house and three around back," I whispered. "Don't know how many left in the vehicles."

Jakub nodded toward the house with a grim face. "Gustaw knows about the courier plane," he whispered. "The Germans have most likely found their dead buddies at the warehouse and your tracks leading from the plane's wreckage."

Two more men exited the lorry and squatted next to the rear tires, smoking.

"They'll squeeze everything they can out of poor Gustaw, then start backtracking from here." A gleam in Jakub's eye caught my attention. "Only thing is, our mines don't know the difference between German boots and ours."

I scratched my neck and felt a tick scurry down my back. "What difference does that make?"

"It will take maybe an hour before they're finished with Gustaw. He'll tell them things, about the trail, about the courier plane, but the Germans are interested in finding us, not land mines, so they won't ask and Gustaw won't tell. They'll find that out themselves. It'll take another hour before they get hold of a metal detector." Jakub squinted at the sun. "It'll be dark by then."

"OK. So where does that get us?"

A pistol shot rang out from the house. A woman screamed.

"Across the road and in the river by midnight." Jakub flinched from the scream. He jutted his chin into the grass off the left side of the trail and probed his fingers slowly down the tall stalks of grass until they touched the ground. "My guess is we only mined the trail and for some distance on either side. Don't know how far, though. We'll have to chance it."

"Shit," I sputtered. "After you, Alphonse."

Jakub worked his way into the grass, using the bayonet to explore the soil and feel for trip wires. After an hour of careful probing, followed by a mad dash in slow motion, we stopped near the verge of the field. We were about three giant steps from the road, far enough to stay concealed from the casual observer.

Another shot came from the house.

We looked back when the officer came through the front door, barking commands. After he holstered his pistol, Jakub grunted when the officer pointed up the trail.

Jakub smiled when we heard the explosion. "Good old Gustaw," he muttered.

Just as Jakub predicted, a car sped off, back the way they had come.

It was dark when the car returned. Fingers of light darted across the field. I was surprised when another foray was organized.

"They really want us bad," I said.

"They don't want us, really, they want revenge," Jakub muttered. "They've lost a squad of men at the plane crash site, Four more at the warehouse, and now another fuck up thanks to Gustaw. Losses like that mean demotions at best, executions more likely. That officer is frantic."

I couldn't see him but I sensed Jakub's smile. "Be ready to jump when they hit the next mine. Your luck is holding out. I hope it gets us to the river."

BOOM! A flash of light and another moment of commotion, people running and shouting, doing things in a panic. We slid into the water without a sound.

"Now what?" I was standing in chest-deep water. A gentle current encouraged me to move down-stream. A waxing crescent moon sat high on the western sky, its light casting a pale glow across the water's surface.

"Keep your head out of the water and your mouth shut," Jakub replied. "You take even a small sip of this shit the best thing that can happen to you is dysentery."

I shuddered. Aside from the occasional shadows of corpses floating across the shaft of moonlight, the river looked clean and beautiful,

Jakub crouched down so only his head and shoulders appeared above the surface. He pointed at a sand bar in the middle of the river. The outlines of a few trees were clumped at one end. "We're gonna walk to that island over there. Slow and easy, don't make a wake. Let the current take you. The river is shallow this time of the year. The only deep part is the channel on the opposite side of the island. We'll deal with that when we come to it."

I stepped into a hole and struggled to regain my footing without making a noise and not gulping water. "Shallow for you, maybe." Grisly thoughts of dysentery danced in my head.

From there on, the journey to the island was a peaceful one. The water temperature was tolerable and, with nothing else to do, I replaced my frantic thoughts about imminent death with the river's pulse as it ebbed and flowed around me. Every step was different. The river bottom changed from sand to gravel to mud, the temperature would drop and climb, the current would speed up and slow down, smells changed with the breeze, from foul to barely tolerable. I was used to the stink now. I felt like I was walking through the heart of a living animal.

Unknown things bumped into me below the surface. I was startled at first, stories I'd heard as a kid about giant, man-eating catfish came to mind. But I assured myself I was safe from the jaws of monsters. Nothing could live in this cesspool.

We crawled up the sandbar's bank just as the eastern horizon showed a hazy blue line of dawn.

"Camouflage yourself next to a tree and sleep," Jakub whispered. He slithered toward the few trees. When I followed him, he turned and shook his head. "Not close together. Find your own place."

That night we lay prone on the sandbar's opposite shore, staring at the rushing water. The channel looked to be a very different story from what we experienced last night.

I'd had a fitful day in between cat naps and hours of insomnia listening to the shooting going on across the channel. Sand fleas and flies kept up their own assault, attacking my eyes, ears and nose. Pissing in the sand didn't help matters. Fortunately, I was so constipated there was no chance of shitting my pants.

When it was finally dark enough to move out from under my hiding place, I was exhausted, and annoyed.

"I'm tired of running," I whimpered.

"I don't blame you," Jakub replied. "I bet the Germans are tired of chasing after you as well."

"That's not the answer I want to hear." I scratched my back where the tick had made its home. "I'm serious, Jakub. If we make it across this impossible obstacle, and that's a big if, then what?"

"We'll make it across, all right. It's the welcoming committee I'm concerned about."

"See? That's just what I'm talking about!" I raised my voice in frustration. "It's one thing after another. Where's the end of this wild goose chase?"

Jakub raised his hand and gestured for quiet. "The end is over there." He pointed at a city block of bombed-out buildings on fire.

I shook my head, exasperated. "Keeping the home fires burning are we?"

Jakub chortled. "Maybe not exactly there, but close by. In the meantime, you are staying here."

He twisted around and crawled back to the trees.

I lifted my head, eyes wide. "Here? What do you mean by here?"

"Shut up and dig." Jakub threw me a stick while he dug furiously from a prone position. "We'll make you a comfortable place."

"Mind telling me what's going on? There's been a change in plans?"

"There's a bend in the river two kilometers downstream. Some quiet water there where I can swim to shore. It's a certainty I would lose you if we went together in the fast water and darkness, so I will return tomorrow night with the means to get us both across safely, along with a more favorable welcoming party."

I lay still and contemplated Jakub's plan. He was right, of course. No way could we both paddle through that churning water and end up on the other side together. Still, I felt abandoned. There was nobody else but Jakub. If he disappeared, died, whatever, I was alone in a very hostile neighborhood. I didn't expect to get out of Warsaw alive, but I did have a shred of hope that I could help my people in some way. I was sure the Allied invasion wasn't going to happen. Or was I? Anyway, the Polish Resistance needed to get my report and make their own decision. That was my mission. But I needed Jakub to make it happen.

Stick in hand, I started digging. "This is going to be my grave, I suppose?"

"Let's call it a modified foxhole. We make it big enough and deep enough for you to stay comfortably concealed."

"Comfortably concealed. I like that. What happens if you don't come back?"

Jakub never stopped digging. "Wait two days. On the third night go back the way we came and wait in Gustaw's farmhouse. Watch for Germans, but I don't think they will return. The Resistance will find you there."

I gulped. "You're not giving me a positive feeling about your new plan."

Jakub grunted. "I'll be back, but it's good to have a plan B."

I had plenty more questions, but I concentrated on digging. Focus on the task at hand, my drill sergeant always told me.

A lot of digging later, Jakub smoothed out the mounds of sand and gravel around the gravesite. He kept looking at his watch and the eastern horizon. The hole was wet at the bottom and the walls were barely stable. It couldn't get any deeper. "Get in and let's see if it fits."

Crawling into a grave is a creepy sensation under any circumstances. It was deep enough to conceal me and long enough for me to stretch out, but I had to be careful not to bump the walls or the whole thing would cave in and smother me. God knows if it would hold up once the sand dried out.

"This whole idea stinks, Jakub." I said, looking up at his stupid grin. The irony of digging my own grave to hide in a place that most assuredly would kill me made me laugh.

"Don't laugh," Jakub smiled. "You'll cause landslides. I will cover you. Then I leave."

I sat up. "Wait! You leaving now?" Rivulets of sand and gravel cascaded around me.

"Time is running short." He dropped his flask and the last slice of black bread into my lap. "Lie down and try not to move too much." He laid some branches over the hole and disappeared, slithering toward the water. His voice trailed off into the distance.

"See you tomorrow night."

Visions

MY GRAVE CAVED IN last night after I woke up and noticed a glow in the sky. I pulled myself up and propped my elbows on the edge to find the source of the glow. It came from Gustaw's house. The place was lit up like a Christmas tree and I doubted it was occupied by the Polish Resistance. That's when the sides of my grave caved in. With all the strength I had left, I pulled myself out of the mound of loose sand and looked around my little kingdom. I finally had to accept the fact I had nowhere to run, nowhere to hide.

The sun seemed to mock me as it came up this morning, my third day on the sand bar. The skinny, pathetic trees laughed and the grass snickered. "He's not coming back, Johnny," they smirked. "What are you waiting for?"

I couldn't have made it back anyway. Too weak to walk unaided, as the day progressed I struggled just to keep up with the pitiful shade the trees afforded as the sun tracked across the hazy sky. I didn't care about the Germans anymore. I'd be grateful if they brought me food and water. Ask me anything, Herr Gruppenführer. I'm at your service.

Fucking, worthless river. I knew it was only a matter of time before I quenched my thirst in its filthy water. I hesitated only because my fear of dying from dysentery still trumped the fear of dying from thirst. I lost my pistol in the cave-in. Didn't matter, it was encrusted with sand and grit, and no longer an option for me to end my ordeal.

The sun's glare burned my face and blurred my vision. Sand fleas were my only companions. I lay on a sandy patch, exposed to the enemy and uncaring, propped up against a tree.

My brother Theo, Number Two, appeared from behind a clump of tall grass. He was wearing a German uniform with bullet holes in the chest. "I ain't shot nobody," he said. "Like you did." He pointed at me. "I told Mama."

I shook my head, my parched lips barely opened. "Don't," I sputtered. "I didn't mean to do it."

Theo laughed his snarky, malicious laugh. "She cried when I told her, Peanut. Said how could my son do such a thing. Ha! I told her how."

I lifted my hand in defense. "Tell Mama... tell Mama I love her, Theo. Please."

Theo and his laughter dissolved. I dropped my arm and closed my eyes in despair until the sound of my name aroused me again. "Jakub?" I said, eyes still closed. "Is that you?"

When I looked up, the silhouette of my brother Albert appeared. He was dressed in an airplane pilot's jumpsuit with a helmet tucked under one arm.

"What I tell you about getting your butt kicked?" Albert stared down at me, his eyes furrowed and a scowl on his face. "You should have stayed with us, little brother. You should have done what I said."

He turned and looked at the smoking remains

of Warsaw. "What a pile of shit. Is that what you're dying for?"

As he stared at the city, I saw the hole in his temple. "I've seen action in the air behind the front lines, defending our country," he said. "What have you been doing?" he added as he, too, dissolved.

I confess I cried, but I was so dehydrated no tears flowed.

A cool breeze passed over me. It smelled of jasmine and rosemary. "There, there, honey." Rosie's voice interrupted my tearless sobs. I covered my face with my hands and shook my head. I was afraid to look.

"No, no," I moaned. "Not you too."

"I miss you, my darling," she said. I breathed in her sweet breath as it wafted across my face.

I opened my eyes. Rosie wore high-heels and a bathing suit, two piece, like what Miss April wore on the wall in Moe's auto shop. Rosie's long brunette hair was pinned up the way Rita Hayworth looked in her publicity photos. Rosie's tummy, shamelessly exposed, gave me a provocative shudder. Her shapely ankles and curvy thighs made me groan.

It had been so long since I'd felt a twinge of desire. I touched my groin.

"I miss you too, Rosie babe. So much."

Rosie smiled and knelt down, her breasts swayed under her top. I stared at her inviting cleavage. "Hurry home, baby," she whispered. "I'm lonely."

The satisfying expansion in my trousers begged for more attention. I tried to stand, but couldn't.

"Stay where you are, baby," Rosie cooed. "How do I look?" She stood and did a seductive pirouette. "Isn't this the cutest bathing suit? I can't wait to wear it for you."

A bruise stained the middle of her back. An

angry purple and yellow splotch with a round, black center.

My penis shriveled. "What's that?" I said.

Rosie turned to face me. Her smile flagged. "Don't you worry about that. It's nothing."

Her image flickered. "I miss your gentle touch," she said, her voice softer now, barely audible.

"Rosie!" I reached out to a ghostly, shimmering vision that dissipated into sparkles. "Don't go!" I pleaded. Dry sobs rose up my throat.

It was time. Time to drink from the Vistula River. To relieve my thirst and release my wretched life.

I was surprised how strong I felt as I roused myself after leaning against the tree all day. I got on all fours. I didn't dare try to stand.

It was afternoon and the sun was low, behind clouds, leaving pools of light on the river.

I made my way to the shallow side of the sand bar and splashed into the water. Despite my intentions, my fear of dysentery kept my mouth and eyes shut while I dipped under the surface. My chapped lips and burned skin tingled with joy as the river washed away sand and fleas and filth.

It felt like a tonic and I didn't look back as the Vistula carried me gently down stream, continuing the journey I had started so long ago. It felt good to be moving again. Raindrops covered the river's surface. I opened my eyes and lifted my face to catch the sweet, clean water.

A line of ducks raced overhead heading upstream. Their urgent, intermittent quacks sounded serious; as though they too, feared the Germans.

A million, billion little hands carried me. They lifted my swollen legs and buoyed my aching arms.

Under such circumstances, even with Jakub gone, I was foolish enough to dare believe my destination would be a welcome one.

The gray outline of a tree-lined riverbank, lit by fires from the burning city, loomed along my left side, getting closer. A damaged bridge appeared in front of me. The sound of rushing water, channeled through the bridge's abutments, echoed across the river. The current accelerated.

I grabbed at the outer fringe of rushes that edged the riverbank, slowing my progress and changing my course landward. Hand over hand and step by step, I pulled through the vegetation and slogged through the mud. I didn't care about noise or commotion. My destination waited for me and that was all I cared about.

On solid ground, I was back on all fours, dripping, leaving a muddy trail behind me. Hunger drove me out of the river. I was hungry in a land that was starving.

A slow climb up an embankment and I rested by the side of the levee road. The Warsaw I saw from the sand bar was farther away, more of a hazy glow now instead of stark outlines of shattered buildings in flame.

Which way? My nose was no help. I couldn't smell grilled sausages in either direction. There were feeble lights in both directions so I picked the one I had been traveling, down river, away from Warsaw.

I clung to the road's gravel shoulder and worked my hands and knees forward, left, right, left, right, searching for food.

I ate two cigarette butts, their charred wood filling reminded me of my friend with no name back in Dresden. I licked a thin slime of butter off the inside of a food wrapper. I chewed on a piece of shoe leather. I washed it all down with a drop of stale beer from the bottom of a bottle.

On the way to my next course, two narrow slits of light appeared ahead of me, accompanied by an engine sound. Judging by the height of the slits off the road, I guessed it was an automobile, not a lorry, and the lights' whitish glare made it German, not Polish. I froze, waiting for the end while the lights swerved toward me, then swayed back onto the road. It missed me by inches, exhaust and gravel flying in my face.

The red tail lights grew bright as the auto came to a stop. Car doors slammed, one, two.

No place to run, no place to hide.

I stared into the glare of flashlights and shook my head at the shrill, high-pitched blather of German questions.

"Private John Zewiski," I said, per Geneva Convention. "RA 29958893."

A blunt force exploded against my temple and little dots of light danced in front of my eyes. I was dragged, then thrown, against the plush upholstery of an auto's rear bench seat and I heard a door slam before I lost consciousness.

"TELL ME HOW IT HAPPENED, comrade Kowalski. I heard you had a kill today. Start from the beginning."

"I was at my post, Commander. Next to the Poniatowski bridge. I was watching traffic using my scope, at the time, because the light was getting dim."

Comrade Kowalski stood in front of his commander's desk. He paused and drew a long drag off his ersatz cigarette. The commander's cramped space was crowded with a line of men standing behind Kowalski. The smell of real tobacco smoke permeated the stuffy room, and Kowalski salivated with envy and desire. Books and papers covered every horizontal space. Posters and communiques covered the walls. The men shuffled and grunted, waiting impatiently for Kowalski to finish so they could take their precious few hours of time off duty.

The commander kept his head down and frowned. He waved his hand. "Yes, comrade, go on."

"An automobile, Mercedes, came on the bridge, moving fast. I was surprised because the Germans never travel alone. It was just the auto. No convoy. It weaved through the bridge traffic, sounding its horn. Very unusual."

The commander slowly looked up from the paperwork scattered across his desk and stared at Kowalski. His tired eyes squinted and he rubbed the stubble that covered his chin. "Unusual indeed. So what happened?"

"Well, I figured it was a courier." Kowalski stiffened, looking at his commander's tired, impatient face. "So I tracked it. I knew I couldn't stop it and I'd reveal my position if I fired, so I followed it to the end of the bridge, just to see where it went."

"Good," the commander nodded. He looked at the line of fidgety men behind Kowalski. "Keep going. I'm waiting."

Kowalski took another drag, dropped the cigarette and snubbed it out with his boot. "The auto got penned in at the tram station, where the square was packed with people, wagons, bicycles. I had it in clear sight even though shadows crossed the open space, so I trained my scope on the auto and waited to see what happened next."

Kowalski paused and the two men waiting behind him quieted and moved closer.

The commander leaned back in his chair and allowed Kowalski a thin smile. "Please, Kowalski, you got our attention. Now get to the point."

"A man in uniform got out of the passenger's side door. It was a German officer, I recognized his hat. He was shouting and waving a pistol. People tried to get out of his way." Kowalski smiled back. "I nailed him at a hundred and fifty meters. Clean shot."

The commander nodded. "What about the driver?"

Kowalski shook his head. "Never saw him. When I left my position a crowd had gathered around the auto and was pulling something out of the back seat."

The man waiting behind Kowalski patted him on the back. "An officer gets you five merits." The man looked at the commander. "That's a hard act to follow," he said.

The commander stood up and pointed at a guard stationed near the door. "Get somebody over there and look the place over. Find out what was in the back seat." He turned back to Kowalski. "Good job, Kowalski. Five merits it is. Same place tomorrow, two floors up. I don't have to tell you they'll be watching for you."

A LOT OF COMMOTION SPOILED MY DREAM. We were out of the car now. My brothers were gone. Rosie held my hand as we looked at the Lehigh River from a grassy riverbank. She was wearing her two-piece swimsuit and we drank lemonade. Kids splashed in the shallow water. "That looks like fun," Rosie giggled.

I stretched out on our blanket. I was surprised because the blanket felt like leather, but I ignored the odd sensation and smiled at Rosie while she watched the kids play. The warm, noon-day sun hid behind her face and traced a golden halo around her hair.

A loud bang interrupted my reverie and Rosie's eyes opened wide in terror. She screamed something in Polish as sour-looking men dragged me off the blanket and pushed me into another place, a dark, enclosed place that smelled of hay and fresh garlic.

I opened my eyes and looked into a cage of quacking ducks. "Welcome aboard," they said. "Care for a kernel of corn?" I politely declined on account of my hands were tied behind my back. A tarp slid down, covering the opening behind me and smothering the noise and commotion that had interrupted my dream. I was moving again. The journey continued.

Flashes of light appeared and disappeared as the ducks and I were trundled over a bumpy track. I didn't know if the light came from behind my eyes or somewhere else. "Where do you think we're going?" I asked.

The ducks quacked in unison. "To the butcher shop!"

We stopped and Polish voices filtered into our space, hushed this time. Whispers almost. The tarp lifted and hands grabbed my legs, dragging me out of my straw bed. "Good bye," I said to the ducks.

"Don't be afraid," they quacked back. "You won't feel a thing."

I cried out when I entered a building while slung over somebody's shoulder. "Not the butcher shop. Please!"

"Cisza!" my tormenters hissed back. They scolded me in Polish as they carried me down stairs, through narrow doorways into a dimly-lit room. I strained to recognize Jakub's voice, but it was not among them.

JAKUB STIRRED AND OPENED HIS EYES when he heard Zewiski's name.

"That's your guy, right? Says so on his identification pendant." A comrade resistance fighter wearing soiled, torn fatigues stood over Jakub's bed. He held Zewiski's dog tag and waited for a response.

Suspended on its chain, the dog tag waved to and fro, glinting in the room's ceiling light.

The tag's movement and its reflection caught Jakub's eye and he sat up, wincing in pain while doing so. "Alive or dead?"

"Most definitely alive. The son-of-a-bitch won't stop jabbering and complaining. He keeps asking about you and his Aunt Elzbieta and says he's got some bad news." The comrade furrowed his brow. "You know what he's talking about?"

Jakub chuckled, jiggling the sling that held his leg above the bed's sheets. "Johnny thinks he's gonna change the world." He gestured toward a water jug and glass sitting on a side table. "Where is he?"

"Stanislaw bunker, Wawer district." The comrade poured Jakub a glass. "He was lucky. A crowd of citizens pulled him out of a German automobile that was hit by one of our snipers. He was unconscious, his hands tied behind his back, wearing Polish fatigues. They hid him in a wagon and brought him to the bunker, undetected. He has a concussion, but besides being a loudmouth pain in the ass, he's OK."

Jakub rubbed the cast that extended from his right thigh to his ankle, trying to relieve the itching that tormented him day and night. He didn't know what was worse, the throbbing ache of his broken femur or the itching. He was told the itching indicated the break was healing, but that didn't stop the agony.

"The commander has been informed about Zewiski's circumstances and wants you to debrief him," the comrade continued. "Your report mentioned you left him alone on a sand bar, but it said nothing about him being captured. He wants to know how he got in that German automobile and why."

Jakub smiled at the comrade. The tension in his face relaxed and he propped himself up against his pillow to drink, letting out a long sigh. "He's alive."

After a long sip of water, Jakub handed back the glass and resumed a serious demeanor. "I need to see him, but give me a day to build up my strength first."

The comrade nodded, returned the glass to the table and stepped back to leave. "You sure one day is enough?"

Jakub waved him off and lay back, clamping his teeth together to keep from moaning. *Johnny's alive. I couldn't get him to Warsaw, so he got the Germans to do it. Clever fellow.*

Vengeance

JAKUB APPEARED TO BE SOUND ASLEEP. Snoring, eyes shut, he faced the ceiling.

"I thought I told you to wait for me." He spoke the moment I peeked in his room. One leg, suspended above the bed covers, swayed from side to side in a cast.

I pulled a chair next to his bed and poured a glass of water from the bedside pitcher. My head throbbed, but the dizzy spells had abated and that terrible taste sensation that comes with a head injury was gone. My thirsty ordeal on the sand bar was still fresh in my mind and I drained the glass.

He looked pretty beat up. Besides the cast, the top of a bandage showed above the neckline of his pajamas. Medicated ointment covered his hands. His face had that strained expression of trying to control pain. His jaw was clenched shut, but I could make out the shadow of a smile in the wrinkles around his eyes.

"Wait for you?" I set down the glass. "While you were catting around all the hot joints in Warsaw? Just didn't seem fair."

Jakub tried to laugh, but coughed instead. He turned and looked at me.

"You missed Marlene Dietrich last night, at the Hotel Polski. She was magnificent."

"Just my luck." I poured another glass. "Hope you said hi for me."

He propped himself up on one elbow, the strain visible in his eyes. A frown interrupted his second attempt to smile. "We've tried to contact your Aunt. Haven't been successful. Her neighborhood took serious damage–"

I put up my hand for him to stop. "One thing at a time. Let's start with you first. What happened?"

It took some prodding, but I finally got it out of him. Jakub broke his leg eluding a German patrol after he got out of the river. Something about climbing a wall and jumping into a dark, unexpected hole on the other side. Once he finished the story he rolled back in his bed, exhausted. "There was no point going back for you with my leg broken," he said. "And when I finally got someone to the sand bar, you were gone."

An orderly came in with a tray of medicines and fresh bandages.

Jakub closed his eyes. "Tomorrow, Johnny. Come back tomorrow. I have some questions..."

The orderly closed the door behind me. Stifled

moans and sympathetic mutterings in Polish came from behind the door as I left.

Jakub's commander bristled when I told him the invasion was cancelled. "The Allies have too much at stake," he said.

"But the raid eliminated any sense of surprise," I countered. "The Germans know what's coming. At best, the invasion will have to be rescheduled and relocated."

Jakub grunted while he weaved on his crutches and his commander laughed. "Invasions don't get rescheduled. Your little mishap at Slapton Sands just means they have to throw more men into combat. Of which they have many."

"Watch the Germans," the commander yelled as Jakub led me out of his bunker. "Tell me when you see more of their butts than their bellies, then we'll know the invasion is underway."

All through the warming month of May, Jakub and I knitted together, him with his broken femur and chest wound and me with my headache and a stubborn case of psoriasis. I think the sand fleas had something to do with that. Our short walks down hallways became longer walks through protected areas of urban rubble.

Jakub got his strength back, but his wounds left him weaker than he once was; he walked with a limp.

I wasn't in great shape myself. The ordeals at Claptown, the smallpox episode, the plane crash and the sand bar had all taken a toll. I wasn't the warrior I once thought I was and I didn't care anymore.

"We shuffle around like two old men," Jakub complained while catching his breath after one of our walks. We sat on the remains of a stairway that led into the bombed-out shell of an apartment building. Broken pieces of furniture and personal effects lay scattered around us. A rat scurried out of a pile of rubble on what was left of the sidewalk; bricks, masonry and tattered pieces of clothing covered worse things I didn't want to know about.

"If only we should live that long." I stared into space, blocking out the carnage, thinking about Rosie.

Jakub slapped me on the back. "You'll change your tune once the Americans arrive."

I shrugged and grunted. "Yeah, I can hear them now. We've missed you Private Zewiski! Please step over here, in front of these six volunteers."

"They wouldn't do that after you've helped liberate Warsaw. You're part of the Polish resistance now."

It was a hopeless idea, but I wondered if the Americans would go soft on me. Let me off with just twenty years hard labor at Leavenworth, maybe. I had stupid fantasies of sitting on the shoulders of jubilant Polish partisans, exclaiming my valor as the Americans rolled into town.

News came in June that the Allies had landed in France. Amid the celebrations, I had to eat some serious crow. Fortunately, Jakub had enough influence to save me from anything worse than finger-pointing and contemptuous looks.

The news was like a tonic. Excitement took the place of despair. Everyone threw themselves into preparing a Polish counter-offensive that was to tie in with the Allies' drive into Germany. The idea was to meet the Allies near the German border and pave their way into Poland before the Russians could reach our eastern flank.

Jakub spent his time at the commander's

bunker and I made myself useful helping with menial tasks. I didn't have much to offer, but it didn't take much Polish to figure out what needed to be done.

"You come with me." Jakub tapped me on the shoulder when he found me stacking sand bags in front of a first-aid bunker.

"I don't think the commander wants to see me," I replied, remembering the look on his face when we first got word about the invasion. "Actually, I've been staying out of his way."

"That's not where we're going."

It was late and I was looking forward to my crust of bread and cup of potable water. My position on the Polish resistance pecking order was not very high, but at least I had a dry place to sleep and token rations, which was a lot more than most of Warsaw's citizens were getting.

I followed Jakub's wobbly pace through an alleyway and up two flights of stairs. Inside a crudely partitioned space, Jakub sat on a mattress and gestured toward a crumbling hole in the wall that used to be a window. A sniper rifle, with scope, leaned against the window's frame.

"We pull guard duty tonight," Jakub said.

I rolled my eyes and sighed. Guard duty. Last time I pulled guard duty at Claptown my life turned upside down.

Jakub ignored me while he crouched next to the window. "I'll take the first watch." He pulled a greasy bag out of his backpack and set a canteen on the floor. "Eat and rest. I'll wake you in four hours."

"I thought you were planning a counter-offensive." I peeked inside the bag and saw two freshly-fried potato pancakes. The aroma was intoxicating. It was hard to concentrate on anything else.

Jakub took a drink from the canteen. "Everyone needs to pull twice their weight. I can do more than sit at a desk. Besides," he broke into a grin, "I miss your company."

"What's that?" I took my nose out of the bag and looked at Jakub.

Jakub shook his head. "I said I've missed you."

I nodded. "I've missed you as well. Too bad we have to socialize in a sniper's nest."

Jakub grimaced as he shifted his injured leg out from under him. He wasn't recovered and I told him so, but no amount of arguing was going to dissuade him from taking on more than his share of duties.

One guard duty led to another through the remainder of summer, 1944.

When the counter-offensive began in August, we were always looking over our shoulders, dodging bullets and listening for signs of Allied advancement, but the Allies never came. Instead, the Russians huddled at our eastern doorstep and waited for the Germans to finish us off.

I remembered Cliff's comment, 'we don't have the numbers,' as our fighting force got smaller and weaker. By mid-September, we knew Warsaw was not going to be liberated by an Allied convoy full of cigarettes and canned hams and chocolate. Churchill and Eisenhower had written off Poland and handed it over to Stalin.

Left to ourselves, with no other options, we kept fighting and dying until one frigid morning in January, the sound of vehicles woke me out of a deep sleep. Eyes wide in anticipation of a miracle I peeked out my window. But instead of friendlies, shot-up German lorries filled the street, heading west. The survivors of the Wehrmacht's Eastern front sat on their dead comrades, stacked under them like cordwood. Those fearsome Germans who for years killed us for sport, stared straight ahead now, ashen-faced, looking as harmless as ducklings.

"Jakub," I muttered, poking the lump of blankets that covered my friend. "The Germans are leaving."

Jakub coughed and stuck his head out from under a pillow. His eyes red and weary from fatigue. "Don't be so sure," he replied.

JAKUB AND I WERE CAPTURED while the remaining Nazi occupying forces were frantically trying to seize everything valuable; especially prisoners, munitions and supplies, and destroy the rest before they high-tailed outta town.

We weren't high-echelon targets. Two Krauts grabbed me while taking a shit outside our surveillance site. I'd trained myself to do the deed early in the morning, just before daybreak, when the German patrols wasted their ammunition on rats and pigeons to keep awake.

When they dragged me into the open, there stood Jakub, with that funny look on his face, between two gray military overcoats. One had a pistol to his head, the other trained a rifle on me.

I smiled back and endured the discomfort of warm shit dripping between my legs. As I hoisted my trousers, I saw the flitting shadows of a backup squad lying in wait. We were not going to be rescued.

"Third time, Johnny," Jakub said as one of the assholes bound my wrists behind my back with wire. "One time too many–"

Before Jakub finished his thought, the asshole with the gun to his head kicked his injured leg and

Jakub fell to his knees with a groan. I hated to see him treated that way.

I knew what he was going to say. Our commander had set up strict rules about hygiene and 'rhythms' as he called it. I knew enough Polish by then to understand his advice. "Never give the enemy the information he needs," he said. "Nobody survives doing the same thing thrice."

There was no time for interrogations, no time for torture. Everyone knew the Russians were on the edge of town. Sappers followed the Germans in the outlying districts, looking for booby traps.

Our group of prisoners rode in the back of a lorry through the town center to the Zoliborz district; what was once a residential neighborhood, with the Vistula river running along one side. I imagined my aunt living there with my uncle and their two kids. Everything clean and tidy, traffic noises up and down the street, vendors pushing their carts, people laughing, chatting... living.

Other lorries followed us into a field next to the river. The men crammed into the cargo beds looked like us. German soldiers swarmed the lorries once they stopped and pushed us out. Like cattle, they herded us to the river bank and spread us into one long rank. Some men stumbled, some resisted. Anyone who fell out of line was shot.

Jakub jostled me toward the right end of the line. "They'll shoot from left to right," he said. "It'll buy us an extra minute," he smirked. "They shoot like they were taught to read in school."

"Ha ha sheesh," I muttered. My whole life had narrowed down to which end of an execution line would last the longest.

I kept my eyes closed as we stood along the

top of the river bank. The wire cut off circulation to my hands and my fingers were numb. The men around us coughed, cried and prayed while I blotted out my circumstances and clung to the memory of my last day with Albert, Theo and the Allentown Army Recruitment office.

"I don't know why they waste the bullets, Johnny," whispered Jakub. "Why don't they just push us off?"

My thoughts of Christmas in Allentown vanished. I opened my eyes, annoyed at the interruption, and frowned at my companion. Jakub's long, greasy hair and tattered fatigues smelled of piss and gun smoke and rancid sauerkraut. I smelled like shit.

"Go ahead and jump," I whispered. "Or do you want their permission first? I'm sure if you turn around and ask politely–"

"Shut up," Jakub hissed.

The man standing on the other side of me chuckled a little too loud. The Kraut sergeant stopped shouting orders. A moment of silence, the sound of steps crunching in the gravel, then a shot split the air around us. The man's head exploded into a pink cloud and he toppled into the river. Bits of him splattered across my face.

I resisted the temptation to lick my lips and, instead, turned my head ever so slightly toward Jakub, "I'm gonna wait my turn and hope a miracle comes first."

"Too bad I don't believe in miracles, Johnny," Jakub mouthed back. "Or I'd give you mine."

Another man let go with a sigh as he peed. A cloud of water vapor wafted up through his trousers and condensed in the cold air.

"Can you imagine my blatant disregard for good manners?" he said defiantly, almost shouting. My Polish isn't great, but I got the message. He followed up his words with a long, profound fart.

Again, deafening silence, followed by more footsteps. They shot him in the back, but off center, wounding him. He spun around.

"Matkojebca!" he shouted, facing the sergeant. His voice cracked while he choked on his own blood. I didn't get the translation but I caught his meaning.

The next round, from a larger caliber weapon I'd never heard before, hit him square in the chest, lifting him off the ground and sending him over the edge. At least this time I didn't suffer any collateral damage.

I looked at Jakub, his jaw clenched, trying not to fall. A shadow of his former self. It was my fault he was here. It was my fault for everything. I owed him my life many times over and this is how I'd paid him back. "Sorry," I said.

The roar of an airplane smothered my apology. Then the sound of rapid, high caliber gunfire hitting the ground. The plane was strafing our vicinity. Strafing us? The Germans? I didn't know.

"Schiesen," the German commander screamed.

Sensing an interruption in the order of things, people bolted from the line. From the frying pan into the fire, prisoners stumbled with their hands behind their backs into crazy, random shooting coming from the air and from the Germans. Groaning and shrieks accompanied the shooting as men crumpled and fell around us.

"Don't move," Jakub said. He spun around with his back behind me. In full panic, the Germans fired randomly into the crowd while Jakub loosened the wire around my wrists.

The airplane made another strafing run and silenced the Germans, but not before they got off one last salvo.

"Now we sail away," Jakub shouted above the roar of the airplane and the cries around us.

With quick, deft movement, he unwrapped the binding, two – three turns. Before he could complete the forth turn, his body jerked against me. Bullets slammed into my back, but Jakub's bulk blunted their momentum and he propelled me forward, to the edge of the embankment.

Jakub gurgled sounds I couldn't understand as he grabbed my wrists and held tight.

A breeze of rancid river air crossed my face and I took a deep breath.

As we toppled over, Jakub's weight rotated us in mid-air and he took the brunt of the impact when we crashed through a crust of ice.

Above me, while we floated, the plane made another pass. A big red star on the fuselage. Russian.

With my head resting on Jakub's beating chest, I struggled with the remaining wire loop. The world grew dark and quiet and we sank below the surface. I thought about my dip in the Baltic and how the Mae Wests protected me as I banged against the ship's hull. Jakub was my protection now, but I had to leave him.

Fingers of cold crept in my chest. I jerked my wrists free while death reached inside me and touched my aching lungs. The strains of a requiem filled my head.

My brothers, Rosie, Kurkowski, my friends lying on the beach at Claptown, Cliff, the man with no name in Danzig, they all chanted while I thrashed and swept my arms and legs, trying to reach the luminous, shimmering surface so far above me. "Join us!" they cried, "Embrace death's warm bosom."

In front of me, Jakub shook his head. His dull, dead eyes stared into mine.

"Live", he said. "Avenge us."

Jim White is a California-based writer of historical and science fiction. He earned an MA in U.S. History. His professional career has included military service, teaching, library science and technical writing. Publications include 'Great Expectations: The Business Correspondence of Gibbons and Lammot, Gold Rush Black Powder Merchants,' *California Historical Quarterly*, 'Unified Field,' *Chronoscope Magazine*, 'Chassy,' The Wapshott Press, and 'Borders In Paradise,' *Adelaide Books*, scheduled to launch October, 2018. More about Jim White can be found at www.myjotting.com

Thank you to the Wapshott Press sponsors, supporters, and Friends of the Wapshott Press.

Muna Deriane

Kathleen Warner

Rachel Livingston

James and Rebecca White

Kit Ramage

Debbie Jones

Steven Acker

Ann Siemens

Suzanne Siegel

Aubrey Hicks

Carol Colin

Ted Waltz

Kathleen Bonagofsky

Cynthia Henderson

Nancy Lilly

Patricia Nerad

Amanda Nerad

Elaine Padilla

Laurel Sutton

Deana Swart

The Wapshott Press is a 501(c)(3) not-for-profit enterprise publishing work by emerging and established authors and artists. We publish books that should be published. We are very grateful to the people who believe in our plans and goals, as well as our hopes and dreams. Our new website is at www.WapshottPress.org. Donations gratefully accepted at WapshottPress.net.

www.ingramcontent.com/pod-product-compliance
Lightning Source LLC
Chambersburg PA
CBHW070224140626
46555CB00018B/1270